"I Thought You Wanted Me To Give You A Chance," He Said.

But why the sudden change of heart? She couldn't escape the feeling that he was up to something. "Of course I do. You just didn't seem too thrilled with the idea."

"My father thinks it would be a good idea for us to get to know one another, and has asked me to be your companion in his absence. I'm to show you and your daughter a good time, keep you entertained."

Oh no, what had Gabriel done? She wanted Marcus to give her a chance, but not by force. That would only make him resent her more. Not to mention that she hadn't anticipated him being so…

Something.

Something that made her trip over her own feet and stumble over her words and do stupid things…like stare at his bare chest.

Dear Reader,

My office is currently under construction, so I'm sitting at my temporary desk (which today is my bed) wondering what I should write about. And feeling, unfortunately, quite uninspired. So I've decided to do another "About Michelle" letter.

Like everyone, I have quirks. Here are a few that my husband has so graciously pointed out for me…

If someone asks me a question, any question, and I don't know the answer, I have to look it up online. And I mean, that very second or it will drive me crazy. I honestly don't know how I managed all those years without Google, or maybe Google is to blame for my obsession. Who knows.

I'm impulsive. Once I make up my mind that I want to do or buy something, I want it *now*. And until I have it/ have done it, I'm obsessed. It's all I can think about. I will spend hours and hours online, searching articles and reviews, looking for the best deal. The internet is my enabler.

And last but not least, I have a *horrible* memory. Tell me your name, and five minutes later I will have forgotten it. I'll forget what I'm saying halfway through a sentence. I'll walk into a room to do something and completely forget why I'm there. I know there are nifty methods to improve memory, which I could probably look up on Google, but…

I'm sorry, what was I saying?

Michelle

MICHELLE CELMER

PRINCESS IN THE MAKING

HARLEQUIN®

entertain, enrich, inspire™

Recycling programs
for this product may
not exist in your area.

ISBN-13: 978-0-373-73188-6

PRINCESS IN THE MAKING

This edition published by arrangement with Harlequin Books S.A.

For questions and comments about the quality of this book please contact us at Customer_eCare@Harlequin.ca.

® and TM are trademarks of Harlequin Enterprises Limited or its corporate affiliates. Trademarks indicated with ® are registered in the United States Patent and Trademark Office, the Canadian Trade Marks Office and in other countries.

www.Harlequin.com

Printed in U.S.A.

Books by Michelle Celmer

Harlequin Desire

Exposed: Her Undercover
  Millionaire #2084
†*One Month with the Magnate* #2099
†*A Clandestine Corporate Affair* #2106
†*Much More Than a Mistress* #2111
  The Nanny Bombshell #2133
  Princess in the Making #2175

Silhouette Desire

  The Secretary's Secret #1774
  Best Man's Conquest #1799
**The King's Convenient Bride* #1876
**The Illegitimate Prince's Baby* #1877
**An Affair with the Princess* #1900
**The Duke's Boardroom Affair* #1919
  Royal Seducer #1951
  The Oilman's Baby Bargain #1970
**Christmas with the Prince* #1979
  Money Man's Fiancée Negotiation #2006
**Virgin Princess, Tycoon's Temptation* #2026
**Expectant Princess, Unexpected Affair* #2032
†*The Tycoon's Paternity Agenda* #2053

Harlequin Superromance

Nanny Next Door #1685

Harlequin Special Edition

No Ordinary Joe #2196

Silhouette Special Edition

Accidentally Expecting #1847

†Black Gold Billionaires
*Royal Seductions

Other titles by this author
available in ebook format.

MICHELLE CELMER

Bestselling author Michelle Celmer lives in southeastern Michigan with her husband, their three children, two dogs and two cats. When she's not writing or busy being a mom, you can find her in the garden or curled up with a romance novel. And if you twist her arm really hard, you can usually persuade her into a day of power shopping.

Michelle loves to hear from readers. Visit her website, www.michellecelmer.com, or write her at P.O. Box 300, Clawson, MI 48017.

To Patti, who has been an invaluable source of support
through some rough times.

One

From a mile in the air, the coast of Varieo, with its crystal blue ocean and pristine sandy beaches, looked like paradise.

At twenty-four, Vanessa Reynolds had lived on more continents and in more cities than most people visited in a lifetime—typical story for an army brat—but she was hoping that this small principality on the Mediterranean coast would become her forever home.

"This is it, Mia," she whispered to her six-month-old daughter, who after spending the majority of the thirteen-hour flight alternating between fits of restless sleep and bouts of screaming bloody murder, had finally succumbed to sheer exhaustion and now slept peacefully in her car seat. The plane made its final descent to the private airstrip where they would be greeted by Gabriel, Vanessa's... it seemed silly and a little juvenile to call him her boyfriend, considering he was fifty-six. But he wasn't exactly her fiancé either. At least, not yet. When he asked her to marry him she hadn't said yes, but she hadn't said no either. That's what this visit would determine, if she wanted to marry a man who was not only thirty-two years her senior and lived halfway around the world, but a *king*.

She gazed out the window, and as the buildings below grew larger, nervous kinks knotted her insides.

Vanessa, what have you gotten yourself into this time?

That's what her father would probably say if she'd had the guts to tell him the truth about this visit. He would tell her that she was making another huge mistake. And, okay, so maybe she hadn't exactly had the best luck with men since…well, *puberty*. But this time it was different.

Her best friend Jessy had questioned her decision as well. "He seems nice now," she'd said as she sat on Vanessa's bed, watching her pack, "but what if you get there and he turns out to be an overbearing tyrant?"

"So I'll come home."

"What if he holds you hostage? What if he forces you to marry him against your will? I've heard horror stories. They treat women like second-class citizens."

"That's the other side of the Mediterranean. Varieo is on the European side."

Jessy frowned. "I don't care, I still don't like it."

It's not as if Vanessa didn't realize she was taking a chance. In the past this sort of thing had backfired miserably, but Gabriel was a real gentleman. He genuinely cared about her. He would never steal her car and leave her stranded at a diner in the middle of the Arizona desert. He wouldn't open a credit card in her name, max it out and decimate her good credit. He wouldn't pretend to like her just so he could talk her into writing his American history term paper then dump her for a cheerleader.

And he certainly would never knock her up then disappear and leave her and his unborn child to fend for themselves.

The private jet hit a pocket of turbulence and gave a violent lurch, jolting Mia awake. She blinked, her pink bottom lip began to tremble, then she let out an ear-piercing wail that only intensified the relentless throb in Vanessa's temples.

"Shh, baby, it's okay," Vanessa cooed, squeezing her chubby fist. "We're almost there."

The wheels of the plane touched down and Vanessa's heart climbed up into her throat. She was nervous and excited and relieved, and about a dozen other emotions too jumbled to sort out. Though they had chatted via Skype almost daily since Gabriel left Los Angeles, she hadn't been face-to-face with him in nearly a month. What if he took one look at her rumpled suit, smudged eyeliner and stringy, lifeless hair and sent her right back to the U.S.?

That's ridiculous, she assured herself as the plane bumped along the runway to the small, private terminal owned by the royal family. She had no illusions about how the first thing that had attracted Gabriel to her in the posh Los Angeles hotel where she worked as an international hospitality agent was her looks. Her beauty—as well as her experience living abroad—was what landed her the prestigious position at such a young age. It had been an asset and, at times, her Achilles' heel. But Gabriel didn't see her as arm dressing. They had become close friends. Confidants. He loved her, or so he claimed, and she had never known him to be anything but a man of his word.

There was just one slight problem. Though she respected him immensely and loved him as a friend, she couldn't say for certain if she was *in love* with him—a fact Gabriel was well aware of. Hence the purpose of this extended visit. He felt confident that with time—six weeks to be exact, since that was the longest leave she could take from work—Vanessa would grow to love him. He was sure that they would share a long and happy life together. And the sanctity of marriage was not something that Gabriel took lightly.

His first marriage had spanned three decades, and he claimed it would have lasted at least three more if cancer hadn't snatched his wife from him eight months ago.

Mia wailed again, fat tears spilling down her chubby, flushed cheeks. The second the plane rolled to a stop Vanessa turned on her cell phone and sent Jessy a brief text, so when she woke up she would know they had arrived safely. She then unhooked the straps of the plush, designer car seat Gabriel had provided and lifted her daughter out. She hugged Mia close to her chest, inhaling that sweet baby scent.

"We're here, Mia. Our new life starts right now."

According to her father, Vanessa had turned exercising poor judgment and making bad decisions into an art form, but things were different now. *She* was different, and she had her daughter to thank for that. Enduring eight months of pregnancy alone had been tough, and the idea of an infant counting on her for its every need had scared the crap out of her. There had been times when she wasn't sure she could do it, if she was prepared for the responsibility, but the instant she laid eyes on Mia, when the doctor placed her in Vanessa's arms after a grueling twenty-six hours of labor, she fell head over heels in love. For the first time in her life, Vanessa felt she finally had a purpose. Taking care of her daughter, giving her a good life, was now her number one priority.

What she wanted more than anything was for Mia to have a stable home with two parents, and marrying Gabriel would assure her daughter privileges and opportunities beyond Vanessa's wildest dreams. Wouldn't that be worth marrying a man who didn't exactly…well, *rev her engine?* Wasn't respect and friendship more important anyway?

Vanessa peered out the window just in time to see a limo pull around the building and park a few hundred feet from the plane.

Gabriel, she thought, with equal parts relief and excitement. He'd come to greet her, just as he'd promised.

The flight attendant appeared beside her seat, gesturing to the carry-on, overstuffed diaper bag and purse in a pile at Vanessa's feet. "Ms. Reynolds, can I help you with your things?"

"That would be fantastic," Vanessa told her, raising her voice above her daughter's wailing. She grabbed her purse and hiked it over her shoulder while the attendant grabbed the rest, and as Vanessa rose from her seat for the first time in several hours, her cramped legs screamed in protest. She wasn't one to lead an idle lifestyle. Her work at the hotel kept her on her feet eight to ten hours a day, and Mia kept her running during what little time they had to spend together. There were diaper changes and fixing bottles, shopping and laundry. On a good night she might manage a solid five hours of sleep. On a bad night, hardly any sleep at all.

When she met Gabriel she hadn't been out socially since Mia was born. Not that she hadn't been asked by countless men at the hotel—clients mostly—but she didn't believe in mixing business with pleasure, or giving the false impression that her *hospitality* extended to the bedroom. But when a king asked a girl out for drinks, especially one as handsome and charming as Gabriel, it was tough to say no. And here she was, a few months later, starting her life over. Again.

Maybe.

The pilot opened the plane door, letting in a rush of hot July air that carried with it the lingering scent of the ocean. He nodded sympathetically as Mia howled.

Vanessa stopped at the door and looked back to her seat. "Oh, shoot, I'm going to need the car seat for my daughter."

"I'll take care of it, ma'am," the pilot assured her, with a thick accent.

She thanked him and descended the steps to the tarmac, so relieved to be on steady ground she could have dropped to her knees and kissed it.

The late morning sun burned her scalp and stifling heat drifted up from the blacktop as the attendant led her toward the limo. As they approached, the driver stepped out and walked around to the back door. He reached for the handle, and the door swung open, and Vanessa's pulse picked up double time. Excitement buzzed through her as one expensive looking shoe—Italian, she was guessing—hit the pavement, and as its owner unfolded himself from the car she held her breath…then let it out in a whoosh of disappointment. This man had the same long, lean physique and chiseled features, the deep-set, expressive eyes, but he was *not* Gabriel.

Even if she hadn't done hours of research into the country's history, she would have known instinctively that the sinfully attractive man walking toward her was Prince Marcus Salvatora, Gabriel's son. He looked exactly like the photos she'd seen of him—darkly intense, and far too serious for a man of only twenty-eight. Dressed in gray slacks and a white silk shirt that showcased his olive complexion and crisp, wavy black hair, he looked more like a *GQ* cover model than a future leader.

She peered around him to the interior of the limo, hoping to see someone else inside, but it was empty. Gabriel had promised to meet her, but he hadn't come.

Tears of exhaustion and frustration burned her eyes. She *needed* Gabriel. He had a unique way of making her feel as though everything would be okay. She could only imagine what his son would think of her if she dissolved into tears right there on the tarmac.

Never show weakness. That's what her father had drilled into her for as long as Vanessa could remember. So she took a deep breath, squared her shoulders and greeted the prince with a confident smile, head bowed, as was the custom in his country.

"Miss Reynolds," he said, reaching out to shake her hand. She switched Mia, whose wails had dulled to a soft whimper, to her left hip to free up her right hand, which in the blazing heat was already warm and clammy.

"Your highness, it's a pleasure to finally meet you," she said. "I've heard so much about you."

Too many men had a mushy grip when it came to shaking a woman's hand, but Marcus clasped her hand firmly, confidently, his palm cool and dry despite the temperature, his dark eyes pinned on hers. It lasted so long, and he studied her so intensely, she began to wonder if he intended to challenge her to an arm wrestling match or a duel or something. She had to resist the urge to tug her hand free as perspiration rolled from under her hair and beneath the collar of her blouse, and when he finally did relinquish his grip, she experienced a strange buzzing sensation where his skin had touched hers.

It's the heat, she rationalized. And how did the prince appear so cool and collected when she was quickly becoming a soggy disaster?

"My father sends his apologies," he said in perfect English, with only a hint of an accent, his voice deep and velvety smooth and much like his father's. "He was called out of the country unexpectedly. A family matter."

Out of the *country?* Her heart sank. "Did he say when he would be back?"

"No, but he said he would be in touch."

How could he leave her to fend for herself in a palace full of strangers? Her throat squeezed tight and her eyes burned.

You are not going to cry, she scolded herself, biting the inside of her cheek to stem the flow of tears threatening to leak out. If she had enough diapers and formula to make the trip back to the U.S., she might have been tempted to hop back on the plane and fly home.

Mia wailed pitifully and Marcus's brow rose slightly.

"This is Mia, my daughter," she said.

Hearing her name, Mia lifted her head from Vanessa's shoulder and turned to look at Marcus, her blue eyes wide with curiosity, her wispy blond hair clinging to her tearstained cheeks. She didn't typically take well to strangers, so Vanessa braced herself for the wailing to start again, but instead, she flashed Marcus a wide, two-toothed grin that could melt the hardest of hearts. Maybe he looked enough like his father, whom Mia adored, that she instinctively trusted him.

As if it were infectious, Marcus couldn't seem to resist smiling back at her, and the subtle lift of his left brow, the softening of his features—and, oh gosh, he even had dimples—made Vanessa feel the kind of giddy pleasure a woman experienced when she was attracted to a man. Which, of course, both horrified and filled her with guilt. What kind of depraved woman felt physically attracted to her future son-in-law?

She must have been more tired and overwrought than she realized, because she clearly wasn't thinking straight.

Marcus returned his attention to her and the smile disappeared. He gestured to the limo, where the driver was securing Mia's car seat in the back. "Shall we go?"

She nodded, telling herself that everything would be okay. But as she slid into the cool interior of the car, she couldn't help wondering if this time she was in way over her head.

She was even worse than Marcus had imagined.

Sitting across from her in the limo, he watched his new rival, the woman who, in a few short weeks, had managed to bewitch his grieving father barely eight months after the queen's death.

At first, when his father gave him the news, Gabriel thought he had lost his mind. Not only because he had fallen for an American, but one so young, that he barely knew. But now, seeing her face-to-face, there was little question as to why the king was so taken with her. Her silky, honey-blond hair was a natural shade no stylist, no matter how skilled, could ever reproduce. She had the figure of a gentlemen's magazine pinup model and a face that would inspire the likes of da Vinci or Titian.

When she first stepped off the plane, doe-eyed and dazed, with a screaming infant clutched to her chest, his hope was that she was as empty-headed as the blonde beauties on some of those American reality shows, but then their eyes met, and he saw intelligence in their smoky gray depths. And a bit of desperation.

Though he hated himself for it, she looked so disheveled and exhausted, he couldn't help but feel a little sorry for her. But that didn't change the fact that she was the enemy.

The child whimpered in her car seat, then let out a wail so high-pitched his ears rang.

"It's okay, sweetheart," Miss Reynolds cooed, holding her baby's tiny clenched fist. Then she looked across the car to Marcus. "I'm so sorry. She's usually very sweet natured."

He had always been fond of children, though he much preferred them when they smiled. He would have children one day. As sole heir, it was his responsibility to carry on the Salvatora legacy.

But that could change, he reminded himself. With a pretty young wife his father could have more sons.

The idea of his father having children with a woman like her sat like a stone in his belly.

Miss Reynolds reached into one of the bags at her feet, pulled out a bottle with what looked to be juice in it and handed it to her daughter. The child popped it into her mouth and suckled for several seconds, then made a face and lobbed the bottle at the floor, where it hit Marcus's shoe.

"I'm so sorry," Miss Reynolds said again, as her daughter began to wail. The woman looked as if she wanted to cry, too.

He picked the bottle up and handed it to her.

She reached into the bag for a toy and tried distracting the baby with that, but after several seconds it too went airborne, this time hitting his leg. She tried a different toy with the same result.

"Sorry," she said.

He retrieved both toys and handed them back to her.

They sat for several minutes in awkward silence, then she said, "So, are you always this talkative?"

He had nothing to say to her, and besides, he would have to shout to be heard over the infant's screaming.

When he didn't reply, she went on nervously, "I can't tell you how much I've looked forward to coming here. And meeting you. Gabriel has told me so much about you. And so much about Varieo."

He did not share her enthusiasm, and he wouldn't pretend to be happy about this. Nor did he believe even for a second that she meant a word of what she said. It didn't take a genius to figure out why she was here, that she was after his father's vast wealth and social standing.

She tried the bottle again, and this time the baby took it. She suckled for a minute or two then her eyelids began to droop.

"She didn't sleep well on the flight," Miss Reynolds said, as though it mattered one way or another to him. "Plus, everything is unfamiliar. I imagine it will take some time for her to adjust to living in a new place."

"Her father had no objection to you moving his child to a different country?" he couldn't help asking.

"Her father left us when he found out I was pregnant. I haven't seen or heard from him since."

"You're divorced?"

She shook her head. "We were never married."

Marvelous. And just one more strike against her. Divorce was bad enough, but a child out of wedlock? What in heaven's name had his father been thinking? And did he honestly believe that Marcus would ever approve of someone like that, or welcome her into the family?

His distaste must have shown in his face, because Miss Reynolds looked him square in the eyes and said, "I'm not ashamed of my past, your highness. Though the circumstances may not have been ideal, Mia is the best thing that has ever happened to me. I have no regrets."

Not afraid to speak her mind, was she? Not necessarily an appropriate attribute for a future queen. Though he couldn't deny that his mother had been known to voice her own very potent opinions, and in doing so had been a role model for young women. But there was a fine line between being principled and being irresponsible. And the idea that this woman would even think that she could hold herself to the standards the queen had set, that she could replace her, made him sick to his stomach.

Marcus could only hope that his father would come to his senses before it was too late, before he did something ridiculous, like *marry* her. And as much as he would like to wash his hands of the situation that very instant, he had promised his father that he would see that she was settled in, and he was a man of his word. To Marcus, honor was not only a virtue, but an obligation. His mother had taught him that. Although even he had limits.

"Your past," he told Miss Reynolds, "is between you and my father."

"But you obviously have some strong opinions about it. Maybe you should try getting to know me before you pass judgment."

He leaned forward and locked eyes with her, so there was no question as to his sincerity. "I wouldn't waste my time."

She didn't even flinch. She held his gaze steadily, her smoky eyes filled with a fire that said she would not be intimidated, and he felt a twinge of…something. An emotion that seemed to settle somewhere between hatred and lust.

It was the lust part that drew him back, hit him like a humiliating slap in the face.

And Miss Reynolds had the audacity to *smile*. Which both infuriated and fascinated him.

"Okay," she said with a shrug of her slim shoulders. Did she not believe him, or was it that she just didn't care?

Either way, it didn't make a difference to him. He would tolerate her presence for his father's sake, but he would never accept her.

Feeling an unease to which he was not accustomed, he pulled out his cell phone, dismissing her. For the first time since losing the queen to cancer, his father seemed truly happy, and Marcus would never deny him that. And only because he believed it would never last.

With any luck his father would come to his senses and send her back from where she came before it was too late.

Two

This visit was going from bad to worse.

Vanessa sat beside her sleeping daughter, dread twisting her stomach into knots. Marcus, it would seem, had already made up his mind about her. He wasn't even going to give her a chance, and the idea of being alone with him until Gabriel returned made the knots tighten.

In hindsight, confronting him so directly probably hadn't been her best idea ever. She'd always had strong convictions, but she'd managed, for the most part, to keep them in check. But that smug look he'd flashed her, the arrogance that seemed to ooze from every pore, had raked across her frayed nerves like barbed wire. Before she could think better of it, her mouth was moving and words were spilling out.

She stole a glance at him, but he was still focused on his phone. On a scale of one to ten he was a solid fifteen in the looks department. Too bad he didn't have the personality to match.

Listen to yourself.

She gave her head a mental shake. She had known the man a total of ten minutes. Was she unfairly jumping to conclusions, judging him without all the facts? And in doing so, was she no better than him?

Yes, he was acting like a jerk, but maybe he had a good reason. If her own father announced his intention to marry a much younger woman whom Vanessa had never even met, she would be wary too. But if he were a filthy rich king to boot, she would definitely question the woman's motives. Marcus was probably just concerned for his father, as any responsible son should be. And she couldn't let herself forget that he'd lost his mother less than a year ago. Gabriel had intimated that Marcus had taken her death very hard. He was probably still hurting, and maybe thought she was trying to replace the queen, which could not be further from the truth.

Looking at it that way made her feel a little better.

But what if he disliked her so much that he tried to come between her and Gabriel? Did she want to go through life feeling like an intruder in her own home? Or would it never feel like home to her?

Was this just another huge mistake?

Her heart began to pound and she forced herself to take a deep breath and relax. She was getting way ahead of herself. She didn't even know for certain that she wanted to marry Gabriel. Wasn't that the whole point of this trip? She could still go home if things didn't work out. Six weeks was a long time, and a lot could happen between now and then. For now she wouldn't let herself worry about it, or let it dash her excitement. She was determined to make the best of this, and if it didn't work out, she could chalk it up to another interesting experience and valuable life lesson.

She smiled to herself, a feeling of peace settling over her, and gazed out the window as the limo wound its way through the charming coastal village of Bocas, where shops, boutiques and restaurants lined cobblestone streets crowded with tourists. As they pulled up the deep slope to the front gates of the palace, in the distance she could see the packed public beach and harbor where everything from sailboats and yachts to a full-size cruise ship were docked.

She'd read that the coastal tourist season stretched from April through November, and in the colder months the tourist trade moved inland, into the mountains, where snowboarding and skiing were the popular activities. According to Gabriel, much of the nation's economy relied on tourism, which had taken a financial hit the last couple of years.

The gates swung open as they approached and when the palace came into view, Vanessa's breath caught. It looked like an oasis with its Roman architecture, sprawling fountains, green rolling lawns and lush gardens.

Things were definitely starting to look up.

She turned to Marcus, who sat across from her looking impatient, as though he couldn't wait to be out of the car and rid of her.

"Your home is beautiful," she told him.

He glanced over at her. "Had you expected otherwise?"

Way to be on the defensive, dude. "What I meant was, the photos I've seen don't do it justice. Being here in person is really a thrill."

"I can only imagine," he said, with barely masked sarcasm.

Hell, who was she kidding, he didn't even *try* to mask it. He really wasn't going to cut her a break, was he?

She sighed inwardly as they pulled up to the expansive marble front steps bracketed by towering white columns. At eighty thousand square feet the palace was larger than the White House, yet only a fraction of the size of Buckingham Palace.

The instant the door opened, Marcus was out of the car, leaving it to the driver to help Vanessa with her things. She gathered Mia, who was still out cold, into her arms and followed after Marcus, who stood waiting for her just inside the massive, two-story high double doors.

The interior was just as magnificent as the exterior, with a massive, circular foyer decorated in creamy beiges with marble floors polished to a gleaming shine. A ginormous crystal chandelier hung in the center, sparkling like diamonds in the sunshine streaming through windows so tall they met the domed ceiling. Hugging both sides of the curved walls, grand staircases with wrought iron railings branched off to the right and the left and wound up to the second floor. In the center of it all sat a large, intricately carved marble table with an enormous arrangement of fresh cut exotic flowers, whose sweet fragrance scented the air. The impression was a mix of tradition and modern sophistication. Class and a bit of excess.

Only then, as Vanessa gazed around in wonder, did the reality of her situation truly sink in. Her head spun and her heart pounded. This amazing place could be her home. Mia could grow up here, have the best of everything, and even more important than that, a man who would accept her as his own daughter. That alone was like a dream come true.

She wanted to tell Marcus how beautiful his home was, and how honored she felt to be there, but knew it would probably earn her another snotty response, so she kept her mouth shut.

From the hallway that extended past the stairs, a line of

nearly a dozen palace employees filed into the foyer and Marcus introduced her. Celia, the head housekeeper, was a tall, stern-looking woman dressed in a starched gray uniform, her silver hair pulled back into a tight bun. Her three charges were similarly dressed, but younger and very plain looking. No makeup, no jewelry, identical bland expressions.

Vanessa smiled and nodded to each one in turn.

"This is Camille," Celia told her in English, in a flat tone that perfectly matched her dour expression, signaling for the youngest of the three to step forward. "She will be your personal maid for the duration of your stay."

Duration of her stay? Were they anticipating that she wouldn't be sticking around? Or more to the point, hoping she wouldn't?

"It's nice to meet you, Camille," she said with a smile, offering her hand.

Looking a little nervous, the young woman took it, her eyes turned downward, and with a thick accent said, "Ma'am."

The butler, George, wore tails and a starched, high collar. He was skin and bones with a slight slouch, and looked as though he was fast approaching the century mark…if he hadn't hit it already. His staff consisted of two similarly dressed assistants, both young and capable looking, plus a chef and baker, a man and a woman, dressed in white, and each looking as though they frequently tested the cuisine.

Marcus turned to George and gestured to the luggage the driver had set inside the door. Without a word the two younger men jumped into action.

A smartly dressed middle-aged woman stepped forward and introduced herself as Tabitha, the king's personal secretary.

"If there is anything you need, don't hesitate to ask,"

she said in perfect English, her expression blank. Then she gestured to the young woman standing beside her, who wore a uniform similar to those of the maids. "This is Karin, the nanny. She will take care of your daughter."

Vanessa was a little uncomfortable with the idea of a total stranger watching her baby, but she knew Gabriel would never expose Mia to someone he didn't trust implicitly.

"It's very nice to meet you," Vanessa said, resisting the urge to ask the young woman to list her credentials.

"Ma'am," she said, nodding politely.

"Please, call me Vanessa. In fact, I've never been one to stand on formality. Everyone should feel free to use my first name."

The request received no reaction whatsoever from the staff. No one even cracked a smile. Were they always so deadpan, or did they simply not like her? Had they decided, as Marcus had, that she wasn't to be trusted?

That would truly suck. And she would have to work extra hard to prove them wrong.

Marcus turned to her. "I'll show you to your quarters."

Without waiting for a reply, he swiveled and headed up the stairs to the left, at a pace so brisk she nearly had to jog to keep up with him.

Unlike the beige theme of the foyer, the second floor incorporated rich hues of red, orange and purple, which personally she never would have chosen, but it managed to look elegant without being too gaudy.

Marcus led her down a long, carpeted hall.

"So, is the staff always so cheerful?" she asked him.

"It's not enough that they'll cater to your every whim," Marcus said over his shoulder. "They have to be happy about it?"

With a boss who clearly didn't like her, why would they?

At the end of the hallway they turned right and he opened the first door on his left. Gabriel told her that she would be staying in the largest of the guest suites, but she hadn't anticipated just how large it would be. The presidential suite at the hotel where she worked paled in comparison. The main room was big and spacious with high ceilings and tall windows that bracketed a pair of paned French doors. The color scheme ran to muted shades of green and yellow.

There was a cozy sitting area with overstuffed, comfortable-looking furniture situated around a massive fireplace. There was also a dining alcove, and a functional desk flanked by built-in bookcases whose shelves were packed with hardback books and knickknacks.

"It's lovely," she told Marcus. "Yellow is my favorite color."

"The bedroom is that way." Marcus gestured toward the door at the far end of the suite.

She crossed the plush carpet to the bedroom and peeked inside, her breath catching. It was pure luxury with its white four-poster king-size bed, another fireplace and a huge, wall-mounted flat screen television. But she didn't see the crib Gabriel had promised.

The weight of her sleeping daughter was starting to make her arms ache, so she very gently laid Mia down in the center of the bed and stacked fluffy pillows all around her, in case she woke up and rolled over. She didn't even stir.

On her way back to the living area Vanessa peered inside the walk-in closet where her bags were waiting for her, and found that it was large enough to hold a dozen of her wardrobes. The bathroom, with its soaking tub and glass-enclosed shower, had every modern amenity known to man.

She stepped back into the living space to find Marcus standing by the door, arms crossed, checking his watch impatiently.

"There's no place for Mia to sleep," she told him, and at his blank expression added, "Gabriel said there would be a crib for her. She moves around a lot in her sleep, so putting her in a normal bed, especially one so high off the ground, is out of the question."

"There's a nursery down the hall."

There was an unspoken "duh" at the end of that sentence.

"Then I hope there's a baby monitor I can use. Otherwise, how will I hear her if she wakes in the middle of the night?" Though Mia slept through most nights, Vanessa was still accustomed to the random midnight diaper changes and feedings, and an occasional bad dream.

He looked puzzled. "That would be the responsibility of the *nanny*."

Right, the nanny. Vanessa had just assumed the nanny was there for the times when Mia needed a babysitter, not as a full-time caregiver. She wasn't sure how she felt about that. Vanessa worked such long hours, and was away from home often. Part of this trip was about spending more time with her daughter.

"And where does the nanny sleep?" she asked Marcus.

"Her bedroom is attached to the nursery," he said, in a tone that suggested she was asking stupid questions. In his world it was probably perfectly natural for the staff to take full responsibility for the children's care, but she didn't live in his world. Not even close. Surely he knew that, didn't he?

She would have to carefully consider whether or not she wanted the nanny to take over the nightly duties. She didn't want to be difficult, or insult Karin, who was probably more than capable, but when it came to Mia, Vanessa didn't fool around. If necessary, she would ask Marcus to move the crib into her bedroom, and if he had a problem with that, she would just sleep in the nursery until Gabriel returned. Hopefully it wouldn't be more than a few days.

"If there's nothing else you need," Marcus said, edging toward the door. He really couldn't wait to get away, could he? Well, she wasn't about to let him off the hook just yet.

"What if I do need something?" she asked. "How do I find someone?"

"There's a phone on the desk, and a list of extensions."

"How will I know who to call?"

He didn't roll his eyes, but she could see that he wanted to. "For a beverage or food, you call the kitchen. If you need clean towels or fresh linens, you would call the laundry...you get the point."

She did, although she didn't appreciate the sarcasm. "Suppose I need you. Is your number on there?"

"No, it isn't, and even if it were, I wouldn't be available."

"Never?"

A nerve in his jaw ticked. "In my father's absence, I have a duty to my country."

Why did he have to be so defensive? "Marcus," she said, in a voice that she hoped conveyed sincerity, "I understand how you must be feeling, but—"

"You have no *idea* how I'm feeling," he ground out, and the level of animosity in his tone drew her back a step. "My father asked me to get you settled in, and I've done that. Now, if there's nothing else."

Someone cleared their throat and they both looked over to see the nanny standing in the doorway.

"I'll leave you two to discuss the child's care," Marcus said, making a hasty escape, and any hope she'd had that they might be friends went out the door with him.

"Come in," she told Karin.

Looking a little nervous, the girl stepped inside. "Shall I take Mia so you can rest?"

She still wasn't sure about leaving Mia in a stranger's care, but she was exhausted, and she would have a hard time relaxing with Mia in bed with her. If Vanessa fell too deeply asleep, Mia could roll off and hurt herself. And the last thing she needed was Marcus thinking that not only was she a money-grubbing con artist, but a terrible mother as well.

"I really could use a nap," she told Karin, "but if she wakes up crying, I'd like you to bring her right to me. She's bound to be disoriented waking up in a strange place with someone she doesn't know."

"Of course, ma'am."

"Please, call me Vanessa."

Karin nodded, but looked uncomfortable with the idea.

"Mia is asleep on the bed. Why don't I carry her, so I can see where the nursery is, and you can bring her bag?"

Karin nodded again.

Not very talkative, was she?

Vanessa scooped up Mia, who was still sleeping deeply, and rolled her suitcase out to Karin, who led her two doors down and across the hall to the nursery. It was smaller than her own suite, with a play area and a sleeping area, and it was decorated gender-neutral. The walls were pale green, the furniture white and expensive-looking, and in the play area rows of shelves were packed with toys for children of every age. It was clearly a nursery designed for guests, and she supposed that if she did decide to stay, Mia would get her own nursery closer to Gabriel's bedroom.

The idea of sharing a bedroom with Gabriel, and a bed, made her stomach do a nervous little flip-flop.

Everything will work out.

She laid Mia in the crib and covered her with a light blanket, and the baby didn't even stir. The poor little thing was exhausted.

"Maybe I should unpack her things," she told Karin.

"I'll do it, ma'am."

Vanessa sighed. So it was still "ma'am"? That was something they would just have to work on. "Thank you."

She kissed the tips of her fingers, then gently pressed them to Mia's forehead. "Sleep well, sweet baby."

After reiterating that Karin was to come get her when Mia woke, she walked back to her suite. She pulled her cell phone out of her bag and checked for calls, but there were none. She dialed Gabriel's cell number, but it went straight to voice mail.

She glanced over at the sofa, thinking she would sleep there for an hour or so, but the bed, with its creamy silk comforter and big, fluffy pillows, called to her. Setting her phone on the bedside table, she lay back against the pillows, sinking into the softness of the comforter. She let her eyes drift closed, and when she opened them again, the room was dark.

Three

After leaving Miss Reynolds's suite, Marcus stopped by his office, where his assistant Cleo, short for Cleopatra—her parents were Egyptian and very eccentric—sat at her computer playing her afternoon game of solitaire.

"Any word from my father?" he asked.

Attention on the screen, she shook her head.

"I'm glad to see that you're using your time productively," he teased, as he often did when he caught her playing games.

And obviously she didn't take him seriously, because she didn't even blink, or look away from the cards on the screen. "Keeps the brain sharp."

She may have been pushing seventy, but no one could argue that she wasn't still sharp as a pin. She'd been with the royal family since the 1970s, and used to be his mother's secretary. Everyone expected she would retire after the queen's death, and enjoy what would be a very generous pension, but she hadn't been ready to stop working. She claimed it kept her young. And since her husband passed away two years ago, Marcus suspected she was lonely.

She finished the game and quit out of the software, a group photo of her eight grandchildren flashing on to her computer screen. She turned to Marcus and caught him in the middle of a yawn and frowned. "Tired?"

After a month-long battle with insomnia, he was always tired. And he wasn't in the mood for another lecture. "I'm sure I'll sleep like a baby when *she* is gone."

"She's that bad?"

He sat on the edge of her desk. "She's awful."

"And you know this after what, thirty minutes with her?"

"I knew after five. I knew the second she stepped off the plane."

She leaned forward in her chair, elbows on her desk, her white hair draped around a face that was young for her years, and with no help at all from a surgeon's knife. "Based on what?"

"She only wants his money."

Her brows rose. "She told you that?"

"She didn't have to. She's young, and beautiful, and a single mother. What else would she want from a man my father's age?"

"For the record, your highness, fifty-six is not that old."

"For her it is."

"Your father is an attractive and charming man. Who's to say that she didn't fall head over heels in love with him."

"In a few *weeks?*"

"I fell in love with my husband after our first date. Never underestimate the powers of physical attraction."

He cringed. The idea of his father and that woman... he didn't even want to think about it. Though he didn't doubt she had seduced him. That was the way her kind operated. He knew from experience, having been burned before. And his father, despite his staunch moral integrity, was vulnerable enough to fall under her spell.

"So, she's really that attractive?" Cleo asked.

Much as he wished he could say otherwise, there was no denying her beauty. "She is. But she had a child out of wedlock."

She gasped and slapped a hand to her chest. "Off with her head!"

He glared at her.

"You do remember what century this is? Women's rights and equality and all that."

"Yes, but *my* father? A man who lives by tradition. It's beneath him. He's lonely, missing my mother and not thinking straight."

"You don't give him much credit, do you? The king is a very intelligent man."

Yes, he was, and clearly not thinking with his brain. No one could convince Marcus that this situation was anything but temporary. And until she left, he would simply stay out of her way.

Vanessa bolted up in bed, heart racing, disoriented by the unfamiliar surroundings. Then, as her eyes adjusted to the dark and the room came into focus, she remembered where she was.

At first she thought that she'd slept late into the night, then realized that someone had shut the curtains. She grabbed her cell phone and checked the time, relieved to see that she had only slept for an hour and a half, and there were no missed calls from Gabriel.

She dialed his cell number, but like before it went straight to voice mail. She hung up and grabbed her laptop from her bag, hoping that maybe he'd sent her an email, but the network was password protected and she couldn't log on. She would have to ask someone for the password.

She closed the laptop and sighed. Since she hadn't heard a word from Karin, she could only assume Mia was still asleep, and without her daughter to take care of, Vanessa felt at a loss for what to do. Then she remembered all the bags in the closet waiting to be unpacked—basically her entire summer wardrobe—and figured she could kill time doing that.

She pushed herself up out of bed, her body still heavy with fatigue, and walked to the closet. But instead of finding packed suitcases, she discovered that her clothes had all been unpacked and put away. The maid must have been in while she was asleep, which was probably a regular thing around here, but she couldn't deny that it creeped her out a little. She didn't like the idea of someone else handling her things, but it was something she would just have to get used to, as she probably wouldn't be doing her own laundry.

She stripped out of her rumpled slacks and blouse and changed into yoga pants and a soft cotton top, wondering, when her stomach rumbled, what time she would be called for dinner. She grabbed her phone off the bed and walked out to the living room, where late afternoon sunshine flooded the windows and cut paths across the creamy carpet. She crossed the room and pulled open the French doors. A wall of heat sucked the breath from her lungs as she stepped out onto a balcony with wrought iron railings and exotic plants. It overlooked acres of rolling green grass and colorful flower beds, and directly below was the Olympic-size pool and cabana Gabriel had told her about. He put the pool in, he'd bragged, because Marcus had been a champion swimmer in high school and college, and to this day still swam regularly. Which would account for the impressively toned upper body.

But she definitely shouldn't be thinking about Marcus's upper body, or any other part of him.

Her cell phone rang and Gabriel's number flashed on the screen. Oh, thank God. Her heart lifted so swiftly it left her feeling dizzy.

She answered, and the sound of his voice was like a salve on her raw nerves. She conjured up a mental image of his face. His dark, gentle eyes, the curve of his smile, and realized just then how much she missed him.

"I'm so sorry I couldn't be there to greet you," he told her, speaking in his native language of Varean, which was so similar to Italian they were practically interchangeable. And since she was fluent in the latter, learning the subtle differences had been simple for her.

"I miss you," she told him.

"I know, I'm sorry. How was your flight? How is Mia?"

"It was long, and Mia didn't sleep much, but she's napping now. I just slept for a while too."

"My plane left not twenty minutes before you were due to arrive."

"Your son said it was a family matter. I hope everything is okay."

"I wish I could say it was. It's my wife's half sister, Trina, in Italy. She was rushed to the hospital with an infection."

"Oh, Gabriel, I'm so sorry." He'd spoken often of his sister-in-law, and how she had stayed with him and his son for several weeks before and after the queen died. "I know you two are very close. I hope it's nothing too serious."

"She's being treated, but she's not out of danger. I hope you understand, but I just can't leave her. She's a widow, and childless. She has no one else. She was there for me and Marcus when we needed her. I feel obligated to stay."

"Of course you do. Family always comes first."

She heard him breathe a sigh of relief. "I knew you would understand. You're an extraordinary woman, Vanessa."

"Is there anything I can do? Any way I can help?"

"Just be patient with me. I wish I could invite you to stay with me, but…"

"She's your wife's sister. I'm guessing that would be awkward for everyone."

"I think it would."

"How long do you think you'll be?"

"Two weeks, maybe. I won't know for sure until we see how she's responding to the treatment."

Two weeks? Alone with Marcus? Was the universe playing some sort of cruel trick on her? Not that she imagined he would be chomping at the bit to spend quality time with her. With any luck he would keep to himself and she wouldn't have to actually see Marcus at all.

"I promise I'll be back as soon as I possibly can," Gabriel said. "Unless you prefer to fly home until I return."

Home to what? Her apartment was sublet for the next six weeks. She lived on a shoestring budget, and being on unpaid leave, she hadn't had the money for rent while she was gone. Gabriel had offered to pay, but she felt uncomfortable taking a handout from him. Despite what Marcus seemed to believe, the fact that Gabriel was very wealthy wasn't all that important to her. And until they were married—if that day ever came—she refused to let him spoil her. Not that he hadn't tried.

The wining and dining was one thing, but on their third date he bought her a pair of stunning diamond earrings to show his appreciation for her professional services at the hotel. She had refused to take them. She had drooled over a similar pair in the jewelry boutique at the hotel with a price tag that amounted to a year's salary.

Then there had been the lush flower arrangements that began arriving at her office every morning like clockwork after he'd flown back home, and the toys for Mia from local shops. She'd had to gently but firmly tell him, no more. There was no need to buy her affections.

"I'll wait for you," she told Gabriel. Even if she did have a place to go home to, the idea of making that miserably long flight two more times with Mia in tow was motivation enough to stay.

"I promise we'll chat daily. You brought your laptop?"

"Yes, but I can't get on the network. And I'll need plug adaptors since the outlets are different."

"Just ask Marcus. I've instructed him to get you anything that you need. He was there to greet you, wasn't he?"

"Yes, he was there."

"And he was respectful?"

She could tell Gabriel the truth, but what would that accomplish, other than to make Gabriel feel bad, and Marcus resent her even more. The last thing she wanted to do was cause a rift between father and son.

"He made me feel very welcome."

"I'm relieved. He took losing his mother very hard."

"And it's difficult for him to imagine you with someone new."

"Exactly. I'm proud of him for taking the change so well."

He wouldn't be proud if he knew how Marcus had really acted, but that would remain hers and Marcus's secret.

"Your room is satisfactory?"

"Beyond satisfactory, and the palace is amazing. I plan

to take Mia for a walk on the grounds tomorrow, and I can hardly wait to visit the village."

"I'm sure Marcus would be happy to take you. You should ask him."

When hell froze over, maybe. Besides, she would much rather go exploring on her own, just her and Mia.

"Maybe I will," she said, knowing she would do no such thing.

"I know that when you get to know one another, you'll become friends."

Somehow she doubted that. Even if she wanted to, Marcus clearly wanted nothing to do with her.

"I left a surprise for you," Gabriel said. "It's in the top drawer of the desk."

"What sort of surprise?" she asked, already heading in that direction.

"Well, it won't be a surprise if I tell you," he teased. "Look and see."

She was already opening the drawer. Inside was a credit card with her name on it. She picked it up and sighed. "Gabriel, I appreciate the gesture, but—"

"I know, I know. You're too proud to take anything from me. But I *want* to do this for you."

"I just don't feel comfortable spending your money. You're doing enough already."

"Suppose you see something in the village that you like? I know you have limited funds. I want you to have nice things."

"I have you, that's all I need."

"And that, my dear, is why you are such an amazing woman. And why I love you. Promise me you'll keep it with you, just in case. I don't care if it's five euros or five thousand. If you see something you really want, please buy it."

"I'll keep it handy," she said, dropping it back in the drawer, knowing she would never spend a penny.

"I've missed you, Vanessa. I'm eager to start our life together."

"If I stay," she reminded him, so he knew that nothing was set in stone yet.

"You will," he said, as confident and certain as the day he'd asked her to marry him. Then there was the sound of voices in the background. "Vanessa, I have to go. The doctor is here and I need to speak with him."

"Of course."

"We'll chat tomorrow, yes?"

"Yes."

"I love you, my sweet Vanessa."

"I love you, too," she said, then the call disconnected.

She sighed and set her phone on the desk, hoping there would come a day when she could say those words, and mean them the way that Gabriel did. That there would be a time when the sort of love she felt for him extended past friendship.

It wasn't that she didn't find him attractive. There was no doubt that he was an exceptionally good-looking man. Maybe his jaw wasn't as tight as it used to be, and there was gray at his temples, and he wasn't as fit as he'd been in his younger years, but those things didn't bother her. It was what was on the inside that counted. And her affection for him felt warm and comfortable. What was missing was that…*zing*.

Like the one you felt when you took Marcus's hand?

She shook away the thought. Yes, Marcus was an attractive man, too, plus he didn't have the sagging skin, graying hair and expanding waist. He also didn't have his father's sweet disposition and generous heart.

When Gabriel held her, when he'd brushed his lips

across her cheek, she felt respected and cherished and safe. And okay, maybe those things didn't make for steamy hot sex, but she knew from personal experience that sex could be highly overrated. What really mattered was respect, and friendship. That's what was left when the *zing* disappeared. And it always did.

Men like Marcus thrilled, then they bailed. Usually leaving a substantial mess in their wake. She could just imagine the string of broken hearts he'd caused. But Gabriel was dependable and trustworthy, and that's exactly what she was looking for in a man now. She'd had her thrills, now she wanted a mature, lasting relationship. Gabriel could give her that. That and so much more, if she was smart enough, and strong enough, to let him.

Four

Marcus was halfway through his second set of laps that evening, the burn in his muscles shaking off the stress that hung on his shoulders like an iron cloak, when he heard his cell phone start to ring. He swam to the side of the pool, hoisted himself up onto the deck and walked to the table where he'd left his phone, the hot tile scorching his feet. It was his father.

He almost didn't answer. He was sure his father would have spoken to Miss Reynolds by now, and she had probably regaled him with the story of Marcus's less than warm welcome. The first thing on her agenda would be to drive a wedge between him and his father, which the king would see through, of course. Maybe not right away, but eventually, and Marcus was happy to let her hang herself with her own rope. Even if that meant receiving an admonishment from his father now. So he took the call.

"Father, how is Aunt Trina?"

"Very sick, son," he said.

His heart sank. He just wasn't ready to say goodbye to yet another loved one. "What's the prognosis?"

"It will be touch and go for a while, but the doctors are hoping she'll make a full recovery."

He breathed a sigh of relief. No one should ever have to endure so much loss in the span of only eight months. "If there's anything you need, just say so."

"There is something, but first, son, I wanted to thank you, and tell you how proud I am of you. And ashamed of myself."

Proud of him? Maybe he hadn't spoken to Miss Reynolds after all. Or was it possible that he'd already seen though her scheme and had come to his senses? "What do you mean?"

"I know that accepting I've moved on, that I've fallen in love with someone new—especially someone so young—has been difficult for you. I was afraid that you might treat Vanessa...well, less than hospitably. But knowing that you've made her feel welcome...son, I'm sorry that I didn't trust you. I should have realized that you're a man of integrity."

What the hell had she told him exactly?

Marcus wasn't sure what to say, and his father's words, his misplaced faith, filled him with guilt. How would he feel if he knew the truth? And why had she lied to him? What sort of game was she playing? Or was it possible that she really did care about his father?

Of course she didn't. She was working some sort of angle, that was how her kind always operated.

"Isn't her daughter precious?" his father said, sounding absolutely smitten. Marcus couldn't recall him ever using the word *precious* in any context.

"She is," he agreed, though he'd seen her do nothing

but scream and sleep. "Is there anything pressing I should know about, business that needs tending?"

"There's no need to worry about that. I've decided to fly my staff here and set up a temporary office."

"That's really not necessary. I can handle matters while you're away."

"You know I would go out of my mind if I had nothing to do. This way I can work and still be with Trina."

That seemed like an awful lot of trouble for a short visit, unless it wasn't going to be short. "How long do you expect you'll be gone?"

"Well, I told Vanessa two weeks," he said. "But the truth is, it could be longer."

He had a sudden, sinking feeling. "How much longer?"

"Hopefully no more than three or four weeks."

A *month*. There was no question that Trina—*family*—should come first, but that seemed excessive. Especially since he had a guest. "A month is a long time to be away."

"And how long did Trina give up her life to stay with us when your mother was ill?"

She had stayed with them for several months in the final stages of his mother's illness, then another few weeks after the funeral. So he certainly couldn't fault his father for wanting to stay with her. "I'm sorry, I'm being selfish. Of course you should be there with her. As long as she needs you. Maybe I should join you."

"I need you at the palace. Since Tabitha will be with me, it will be up to you to see that Vanessa and Mia have anything they need."

"Of course." He could hardly wait.

"And I know this is a lot to ask, but I want you to keep them entertained."

Marcus hoped he didn't mean that the way it sounded. *"Entertained?"*

"Make them feel welcome. Take them sightseeing, show them a good time."

The idea had been to stay away from her as much as humanly possible, not be her tour guide. "Father—"

"I realize I'm asking a lot of you under the circumstances, and I know it will probably be a bit awkward at first, but it will give you and Vanessa a chance to get to know one another. She's truly a remarkable woman, son. I'm sure that once you get to know her you'll love her as much as I do."

Nothing his father could say would make Marcus want to spend time with that woman. And no amount of time that he spent with her would make him "love" her. "Father, I don't think—"

"Imagine how she and her daughter must feel, in a foreign country where they don't know a soul. And I feel terrible for putting her in that position. It took me weeks to convince her to come here. If she leaves, she may never agree to come back."

And that would be a bad thing?

Besides, Marcus didn't doubt for an instant that she had just been playing hard to get, stringing his father along, and now that she was here, he seriously doubted she had any intention of leaving, for any reason. But maybe in this case absence wouldn't make the heart grow fonder. Maybe it would give his father time to think about his relationship with Miss Reynolds and realize the mistake he was making.

Or maybe, instead of waiting for this to play out, Marcus could take a more proactive approach. Maybe he could persuade her to leave.

The thought brought a smile to his face.

"I'll do it," he told his father.

"I have your word?"

"Yes," he said, feeling better about the situation already. "You have my word."

"Thank you, son. You have no idea how much this means to me. And I don't want you to worry about anything else. Consider yourself on vacation until I return."

"Is there anyplace in particular you would like me to take her?"

"I'll email a list of the things she might enjoy doing."

"I'll watch for it," he said, feeling cheerful for the first time in weeks, since his father had come home acting like a lovesick teenager.

"She did mention a desire to tour the village," the king said.

That was as good a place to start as any. "Well then, we'll go first thing tomorrow."

"I can't tell you what a relief this is. And if ever you should require anything from me, you need only ask."

Send her back to the U.S., he wanted to say, but he would be taking care of that. After he was through with her, she would be *sprinting* for the plane. But the key with a woman like her was patience and subtlety.

He and his father hung up, and Marcus dropped his phone back on the table. He looked over at the pool, then up to the balcony of Miss Reynolds's room. He should give her the good news right away, so she would have time to prepare for tomorrow's outing. He toweled off then slipped his shirt, shorts and sandals on, combing his fingers through his wet hair as he headed upstairs. He half expected to hear her daughter howling as he approached her room, but the hallway was silent.

He knocked, and she must have been near the door because it opened almost immediately. She had changed into snug black cotton pants, a plain pink T-shirt, and her hair was pulled up in a ponytail. She looked even younger this way, and much more relaxed than she had when she stepped off the plane. It struck him again how attractive she really was. Without makeup she looked a little less exotic and vampy, but her features, the shape of her face, were exquisite.

He looked past her into the suite and saw that she had spread a blanket across the carpet in the middle of the room. Mia was in the center, balanced on her hands and knees, rocking back and forth, shaking her head from side to side, a bit like a deranged pendulum. Then she stopped, toppled over to the left, and rolled onto her back, looking dazed.

Was she having some sort of fit or seizure?

"Is she okay?" Marcus asked, wondering if he should call the physician.

Miss Reynolds smiled at her daughter. "She's fine."

"What was she doing?" Marcus asked.

"Crawling."

Crawling? "She doesn't seem to be getting very far."

"Not yet. The first step is learning to balance on her hands and knees."

She apparently had a long way to go to master that.

Mia squealed and rolled over onto her tummy, then pushed herself back up and resumed rocking. She seemed to be doing all right, until her arms gave out and she pitched forward. Marcus cringed as she fell face-first into the blanket, landing on her button nose. She lifted her head, looking stunned for a second, then she screwed up her face and started to cry.

When Miss Reynolds just stood there, Marcus asked, "Is she okay?"

"She's probably more frustrated than injured."

After several more seconds of Mia wailing, when she

did nothing to comfort the child, he said, "Aren't you going to pick her up?"

She shrugged. "If I picked her up every time she got discouraged, she'd never learn to try. She'll be fine in a second."

No sooner had she spoken the words than Mia's cries abruptly stopped, then she hoisted herself back up on her hands and knees, starting the process all over again. Rocking, falling over, wailing…

"Does she do this often?" he asked after watching her for several minutes.

She sighed, as if frustrated, but resigned. "Almost constantly for the past three days."

"Is that…normal?"

"For her it is. She's a very determined child. She'll keep doing something over and over until she gets it right. She gets that from my father, I think."

He could tell, from the deep affection in her eyes, the pride in her smile as she watched her daughter, that Miss Reynolds loved the little girl deeply. Which made her attempts to con his father all the more despicable.

"I'm sorry," she said, finally turning to him. "Was there something you wan…" She trailed off, blinking in surprise as she took in the sight of him, as if she just now noticed how he was dressed. Starting at his sandals, her eyes traveled up his bare legs and over his shorts, then they settled on the narrow strip of chest where the two sides of his shirt had pulled open. For several seconds she seemed transfixed, then she gave her head a little shake, and her eyes snapped up to his.

She blinked again, looking disoriented, and asked, "I'm sorry, what did you say?"

He began to wonder if maybe he'd been mistaken earlier, and she really was a brainless blonde. "I didn't say anything. But I believe you were about to ask me if there was something that I wanted."

Her cheeks blushed bright pink. "You're right, I was. Sorry. Was there? Something you wanted, I mean."

"If you have a moment, I'd like to have a word with you."

"Of course," she said, stepping back from the door and pulling it open, stumbling over her own foot. "Sorry. Would you like to come in?"

He stepped into the room, wondering if perhaps she'd been sampling the contents of the bar. "Are you all right?"

"I took a nap. I guess I'm not completely awake yet. Plus, I'm still on California time. It's barely seven a.m. in Los Angeles. Technically I was up most of the night."

That could explain it, he supposed, yet he couldn't help questioning her mental stability.

She closed the door and turned to him. "What did you want to talk about?"

"I want to know why you lied to my father."

She blinked in surprise, opened her mouth to speak, then shut it again. Then, as if gathering her patience, she took a deep breath, slowly blew it out, and asked, "Refresh my memory, what did I lie about?"

Did she honestly not know what he meant, or were there so many lies, she couldn't keep track? "You told my father that I made you feel welcome. We both know that isn't true."

She got an "oh *that*" look on her face. "What was I supposed to tell him? His son, who he loves and respects dearly, acted like a big jer—" She slapped a hand over her mouth, but it was pretty obvious what she'd been about to say.

Marcus had to clench his jaw to keep it from falling open. "Did you just call me a *jerk?*"

She shook her head, eyes wide. "No."

"Yes, you did. You called me a *big jerk*."

She hesitated, looking uneasy. "Maybe I did."

"Maybe?"

"Okay, I did. I told you, I'm half asleep. It just sort of… slipped out. And let's be honest, Marcus, you were acting like a jerk."

He was sure people said unfavorable things about him all the time, but no one, outside of his family, had ever dared insult him to his face. Twice. He should feel angry, or annoyed, yet all he felt was an odd amusement. "Are you *trying* to make me dislike you?"

"You already don't like me. At this point I doubt anything I say, or don't say, will change that. Which I think is kind of sad but…" She shrugged. "And for the record, I didn't *lie* to Gabriel. I just…fudged the truth a little."

"Why?"

"He has enough on his mind. He doesn't need to be worrying about me. Besides, I can fight my own battles."

If he didn't know better, he might believe that she really did care about his father. But he knew her type. He'd dated a dozen women just like her. She was only after one thing—his legacy—and like the others, he would make sure that she never got her hands on it.

"I would hardly call this a battle," he told her.

She folded her arms, emphasizing the fullness of her breasts. "You would if you were me."

Marcus had to make an effort to keep his eyes on her face. But even that was no hardship. She was exceptionally attractive and undeniably sexy. A beautiful woman with a black heart.

Her eyes wandered downward, to his chest, lingering there for several seconds, then as if realizing she was staring, she quickly looked away.

She didn't strike him as the type to be shy about the male physique. Or maybe it was just his that bothered her.

"Look," she said. "You don't like me, and that's fine. I can even understand why. It's disappointing that you aren't going to give me a chance, but, whatever. And if I'm being totally honest, I'm not so crazy about you either. So why don't we just agree to stay out of each other's way?"

"Miss Reynolds—"

"It's *Vanessa*. You could at least have the decency to use my first name."

"*Vanessa*," he said. "How would you feel if we called a truce?"

Five

A truce?

Vanessa studied Marcus's face, trying to determine if his words were sincere. Instead, all she could seem to concentrate on was his damp, slicked-back hair and the single wavy lock that had fallen across his forehead. She felt the strongest urge to brush it back with her fingers. And why couldn't she stop looking at that tantalizing strip of tanned, muscular, bare chest?

"Why would you do that?" she asked, forcing her attention above his neck. He folded his arms over his chest and she had to wonder if he'd seen her staring. Was she creeping him out? If she were him, she would probably be creeped out.

"I thought you wanted me to give you a chance," he said.

But why the sudden change of heart? A couple of hours ago he could barely stand to be in the same room with her. She couldn't escape the feeling that he was up to something. "Of course I do, you just didn't seem too thrilled with the idea."

"That was before I learned that for the next few weeks, we're going to be seeing a lot of each other."

She blinked. "What do you mean?"

"My father thinks it would be a good idea for us to get to know one another, and in his absence has asked me to be your companion. I'm to show you and your daughter a good time, keep you entertained."

Oh no, what had Gabriel done? She wanted Marcus to give her a chance, but not by force. That would only make him resent her more. Not to mention that she hadn't anticipated him being so...

Something.

Something that made her trip over her own feet and stumble over her words, and do stupid things like stare at his bare chest and insult him to his face.

"I don't need a companion," she told him. "Mia and I will be fine on our own."

"For your safety, you wouldn't be able to leave the palace without an escort."

"My safety?"

"There are certain criminal elements to consider."

Her heart skipped a beat. "What kind of criminal elements?"

"The kind who would love nothing more than to get their hands on the future queen. You would fetch quite the ransom."

She couldn't decide if he was telling the truth, or just trying to scare her. Kidnappings certainly weren't unheard of, but Vareo was such a quiet, peaceful country. No handguns, very little crime. Gabriel hadn't mentioned any potential threat or danger.

And why would he when he was trying to convince

her to marry him? There was a reason royalty had body-guards, right?

Wait a minute. Who even knew that she was here? It wasn't as if Gabriel would broadcast to the country that eight months after his wife's death he was bringing his new American girlfriend in for a visit.

Would he?

"The point is," Marcus said, "my father wanted you to have an escort, and that person is me."

"What about Tabitha?"

"She's flying to Italy to be with my father. He takes her everywhere. Some people have even thought…" He paused and shook his head. "Never mind."

Okay, now he *was* trying to mess with her.

But how well do you really know Gabriel, that annoying voice of doubt interjected. He could have a dozen mistresses for all she knew. Just because he claimed to have been faithful to his wife didn't mean it was true. Maybe there was no sick sister-in-law. Maybe he was with another one of his girlfriends. Maybe there had been a scheduling conflict and he chose her over Vanessa. Maybe he—

Ugh! What are you doing?

She *trusted* Gabriel, and she hated that Marcus could shake her faith with one simple insinuation. And a ridiculous one at that. Maybe she hadn't known Gabriel long, but in that short time he had never been anything but honest and dependable. And until someone produced irrefutable evidence to the contrary, she was determined to trust him.

This wasn't another dumb mistake.

It wasn't Gabriel's fault that she'd had lousy luck with relationships, and it wasn't fair to judge him on her own bad experiences. If he wanted her to spend a couple of weeks getting to know his son, that's what she would do, even if she didn't exactly trust Marcus, and questioned his motives. She would just be herself, and hope that Marcus would put aside his doubts and accept her.

"I guess I'm stuck with you then," she told him.

Marcus frowned, looking as if she'd hurt his feelings. "If the idea of spending time with me is so offensive—"

"No! Of course not. That isn't what I meant." No matter what she said, it always seemed to be the wrong thing. "I really would like us to get acquainted, Marcus. I just don't want you to feel pressured, as if you have no choice. I can only imagine how awkward this is for you, and how heartbreaking it was to lose your mother. It sounds as if she was a remarkable woman, and I would never in a million years try to replace her, or even think that I could. I just want Gabriel to be happy. He deserves it. I think that would be much more likely to happen if you and I are friends. Or at the very least, not mortal enemies."

"I'm willing to concede that I may have rushed to judgment," he said. "And for the record, my father is not *forcing* me. I could have refused, but I know it's important to him."

It was no apology for his behavior earlier, but it was definitely a start. And she hoped he really meant it, that he didn't have ulterior motives for being nice to her. "In that case, I would be honored to have you as my escort."

"So, truce?" he said, stepping closer with an outstretched hand. And boy did he smell good. Some sort of spicy delicious scent that made her want to bury her face in his neck and take a big whiff.

No, she *definitely* didn't want to do that. And she didn't want to feel the zing of awareness when he clasped her hand, the tantalizing shiver as his thumb brushed across the top of her hand, or the residual buzz after he let go.

How could she zing for a man she didn't even like?

"My father will be sending me a list of activities he thinks you'll enjoy, and he's asked me to accompany you to the village tomorrow. If there's anything in particular you'd like to do, or someplace you would like to see, let me know and we'll work it into the schedule."

Honestly, she would be thrilled to just lie around by the pool and doze for a week, but she knew Gabriel wanted her to familiarize herself with the area, because how could she decide if she wanted to live somewhere if she didn't see it? "If there's anything I'll let you know."

"Be ready tomorrow at ten a.m."

"I will."

He nodded and walked out, closing the door behind him.

Vanessa sat on the floor beside her daughter, who had tired of rocking, and was now lying on her tummy gnawing contentedly on a teething ring.

The idea of spending so much time alone with Marcus made her uneasy, but she didn't seem to have much choice. To refuse would only hurt Gabriel's feelings, and make her look like the bad guy. At the very least, when the staff saw that Marcus was accepting her, they might warm up to her as well.

Vanessa's cell phone rang and she jumped up to grab it off the desk, hoping it was Gabriel.

It was her best friend Jessy.

"Hey! I just woke up and got your text," Jessy said, and Vanessa could picture her, sitting in bed in her pajamas, eyes puffy, her spiky red hair smashed flat from sleeping with the covers pulled over her head. "How was the flight?"

"A nightmare. Mia hardly slept." She smiled down at her daughter who was still gnawing and drooling all over the blanket. "But she seems to be adjusting pretty well now."

"Was Gabriel happy to see you?"

Vanessa hesitated. She didn't want to lie to Jessy, but she was afraid the truth would only add to her friend's doubts. But if she couldn't talk to her best friend, who could she talk to?

"There was a slight change of plans." She explained the situation with Gabriel's sister-in-law, and why he felt he had to be with her. "I know what you're probably thinking."

"Yes, I have reservations about you taking this trip, but I have to trust that you know what's best for you and Mia."

"Even if you don't agree?"

"I can't help but worry about you, and I absolutely hate the idea of you moving away. But ultimately, what I think doesn't matter."

To Vanessa it did. They had been inseparable since Vanessa moved to L.A. With her statuesque figure and exquisitely beautiful features—assets that, unlike Vanessa, she chose to cleverly downplay—Jessy understood what it was like to be labeled the "pretty" girl. She knew that, depending on the circumstances, it could be more of a liability than an asset. They also shared the same lousy taste in men, although Jessy was now in a relationship with Wayne, a pharmaceutical rep, who she thought might possibly be the *one*. He was attractive without being too handsome—since she'd found most of the really good-looking guys to be arrogant—he had a stable career, drove a nice car and lived in an oceanside condo. And aside from the fact that he had a slightly unstable and bitter ex-wife and a resentful teenaged daughter with self-cutting issues in Seattle, he was darn close to perfect.

Vanessa hoped that they had both found their forever man. God knows they had paid their dues.

"So, what will you do until Gabriel comes back?" Jessy asked, and Vanessa heard the whine of the coffee grinder in the background.

"His son has agreed to be my companion." Just the thought caused a funny little twinge in her stomach.

"Companion?"

"He'll take me sightseeing, keep me entertained."

"Is he as hot in person as he is in the photos you showed me?"

Unfortunately. "On a scale of one to ten, he's a solid fifteen."

"So, if things don't work out with Gabriel…" she teased.

"Did I mention that he's also a jerk? And he doesn't seem to like me very much. Not that I don't understand why." She picked a hunk of carpet fuzz from Mia's damp fingers before she could stuff it in her mouth. "Gabriel wants us to be friends. But I think I would settle for Marcus not hating my guts."

"Vanessa, you're one of the sweetest, kindest, most thoughtful people I've ever met. How could he not like you?"

The problem was, sometimes she was too nice and too sweet and too thoughtful. To the point that she let people walk all over her. And Marcus struck her as the sort of man who would take advantage of that.

Or maybe she was being paranoid.

"He's very…intense," she told Jessy. "When he steps into a room he's just so…*there*. It's a little intimidating."

"Well, he is a prince."

"And Gabriel is a king, but I've never felt anything but comfortable with him."

"Don't take this the wrong way, but maybe Gabriel, being older, is more like…a father figure."

"Jessy, my dad has been enough of a father figure to last a dozen lifetimes."

"And you've told me a million times how his criticism makes you feel like a failure."

She couldn't deny that, and Gabriel's lavish attention did make her feel special, but she wasn't looking for a substitute father. Quite the opposite in fact. In the past she always found herself attracted to men who wanted to control or dominate her. And the worst part was that she usually let them. This time she wanted a partner. An *equal*.

Maybe the main thing that bothered her about Marcus—besides the fact that he despised her—was that he seemed a bit too much like the sort of man she used to date.

"I don't trust Marcus," she told Jessy. "He made it clear the minute I stepped off the plane that he didn't like me, then a couple of hours later he was offering to take me sightseeing. He said he's doing it for his father, but I'm not sure I buy that. If he really wanted to please Gabriel, wouldn't he have been nice to me the second I stepped off the plane?"

"Do you think he's going to try to come between you and Gabriel?"

"At this point, I'm not sure what to think." The only thing she did know was that something about Marcus made her nervous, and she didn't like it, but she was more or less stuck with him until Gabriel returned.

"I have some good news of my own," Jessy said. "Wayne has invited me to Arkansas for a couple of days for his parents' fortieth anniversary party. He wants me to meet his family."

"You're going, right?"

"I'd love to. Do you realize how long it's been since I've met a man's family, since I've even wanted to? The thing is, they live in a remote area that doesn't have great cell coverage and I might be hard to get ahold of. I'm just a little worried that if you end up needing me—"

"Jessy, I'll be fine. Worst-case scenario, I can call my dad." Although things would have to be pretty awful for her to do that.

"Are you sure? I know you say everything is okay, but I still worry about you."

"Well, don't," she told Jessy. "I can handle Prince Marcus."

She just hoped that was true.

Six

Marcus was sure he had Vanessa pegged, but after spending a day with her in the village, he was beginning to wonder if his original assumptions about her were slightly, well…unreliable.

His first hint that something might be off was when he arrived at her door at 10 a.m. sharp, fully anticipating a fifteen- or twenty-minute wait while she finished getting ready. It was a game women liked to play. They seemed to believe it drew out the anticipation or gave them power, or some such nonsense, when in reality, it just annoyed him. But when Vanessa opened the door dressed in conservative cotton shorts, a sleeveless top, comfortable-looking sandals and a floppy straw hat, she was clearly ready to go, and with a camera hanging from a strap around her neck, a diaper bag slung over one shoulder and her daughter on her hip, she looked more like an American tourist than a gold digger angling for the position of queen.

His suspicions grew throughout the day while he witnessed her shopping habits—or lack thereof. Tabitha, with only the king's best interest at heart, had warned Marcus of the credit card his father had requested for Vanessa, and its outrageous credit limit. Therefore, Marcus requested his driver be at the ready in anticipation of armfuls of packages. But by midafternoon they had visited at least a dozen shops showcasing everything from souvenirs to designer clothing to fine jewelry, and though he'd watched her admire the fashions, and seen her gaze longingly at a pair of modestly priced, hand-crafted earrings, all she'd purchased was a T-shirt for her daughter, a postcard that she said she intended to send to her best friend in L.A. and a paperback romance novel—her one guilty pleasure, she'd explained with a wry smile. And she'd paid with cash. He had an even bigger surprise when he heard her speaking to a merchant and realized she spoke his language fluently.

"You never mentioned that you could speak Variean," he said, when they left the shop.

She just shrugged and said, "You never asked."

She was right. And everything about her puzzled him. She was worldly and well traveled, but there was a childlike delight and curiosity in her eyes with each new place she visited. She didn't just see the sights, but absorbed her surroundings like a sponge, the most trivial and mundane details—things he would otherwise overlook—snagging her interest. And she asked a million questions. Her excitement and enthusiasm were so contagious he actually began to see the village with a fresh pair of eyes. Even though they were tired and achy from lack of sleep.

She was intelligent, yet whimsical, and at times even a little flighty. Poised and graceful, yet adorably awkward, occasionally bumping into a store display or another shopper, or tripping on a threshold—or even her own feet.

Once, she was so rapt when admiring the architecture of a historical church, she actually walked right into a tourist who had paused abruptly in front of her to take a photo. But instead of looking annoyed, Vanessa simply laughed, apologized and complimented the woman on her shoes.

Vanessa also had an amusing habit of saying exactly what she was thinking, while she was thinking it, and oftentimes embarrassing herself or someone else in the process.

Though she was obviously many things—or at least wanted him to believe she was—if he had to choose a single word to describe her it would probably be…*quirky*.

Twenty-four hours ago he would have been content never to see her again. But now, as he sat across from her on a blanket in the shade of an olive tree near the dock, in the members-only park off the marina, watching her snack on sausage, cheese and crackers—which she didn't eat so much as inhale—with Mia on the blanket between them rocking back and forth, back and forth on her hands and knees, he was experiencing a disconcerting combination of perplexity, suspicion and fascination.

"I guess you were hungry," he said as she plucked the last cheese wedge from the plate and popped it in her mouth.

Most women would be embarrassed or even offended by such as observation, but she just shrugged.

"I'm borderline hypoglycemic, so I have to eat at least five or six times a day. But I was blessed with a fast metabolism, so I never gain weight. It's just one more reason for other women to hate me."

"Why would other women hate you?"

"Are you kidding? A woman who looks like I do, who can eat anything and not gain an ounce? Some people consider that an unforgivable crime, as though I have some sort of control over how pretty I am, or how my body processes nutrients. You have no idea how often as a teenager I wished I were more ordinary."

Acknowledging her own beauty should have made her come off as arrogant, but she said it with such disdain, so much self-loathing, he actually felt a little sorry for her.

"I thought all women wanted to be beautiful," he said.

"Most do, they just don't want *other* women to be beautiful too. They don't like competition. I was popular, so I had no real friends."

That made no sense. "How could you be popular if you had no friends?"

She took a sip of her bottled water than recapped it. "I'm sure you know the saying, keep your friends close and your enemies closer."

"And you were the enemy?"

"Pretty much. Those stereotypes you see in movies about popular girls aren't as exaggerated as you might think. They can be vicious."

Mia toppled over and wound up lying on her back against his leg. She smiled up at him and gurgled happily, and he couldn't help but smile back. He had the feeling she was destined to be as beautiful as her mother.

"So, if the popular girls were so terrible, why didn't you make friends who weren't popular?"

"Girls were intimidated by me. It took them a long time to get past my face to see what was on the inside. And just when they would begin to realize that I wasn't a snob, and I started to form attachments, my dad would uproot us again and I'd have to start over in a new school."

"You moved often?"

"At least once a year, usually more. My dad's in the army."

He had a difficult time picturing that. He'd imagined

her as being raised in an upscale suburban home, with a pampered, trophy wife mother and an executive father who spoiled her rotten. Apparently he'd been wrong about many things.

"How many different places have you lived?" he asked.

"Too many. The special weapons training he did meant moving a lot. Overseas we were based in Germany, Bulgaria, Israel, Japan and Italy, and domestically we lived in eight different states at eleven bases. All by the time I was seventeen. Deep down, I think all the moving was just his way of coping with my mom's death."

The fact that she, too, had lost her mother surprised him. "When did she die?"

"I was five. She had the flu of all things."

His mother's death, the unfairness of it, had left him under a cloud so dark and obliterating, he felt as if he would never be cheerful again. Yet Vanessa seemed to maintain a perpetually positive attitude and sunny disposition.

"She was only twenty-six," Vanessa said.

"That's very young."

"It was one of those fluke things. She just kept getting worse and worse, and by the time she went in for treatment, it had turned into pneumonia. My dad was away at the time, stationed in the Persian Gulf. I don't think he ever forgave himself for not being there."

At least Marcus had his mother for twenty-eight years. Not that it made losing her any easier. And though he knew it happened all the time, it still struck him as terribly unjust for a child to lose a parent so young, and from such a common and typically mild affliction.

"How about you?" she asked. "Where have you lived?"

"I've visited many places," Marcus said, "but I've never lived anywhere but the palace."

"Haven't you ever wanted to be independent? Out on your own?"

More times than he could possibly count. When people heard *royalty,* they assumed a life of grandeur and excess, but the responsibilities attached to the crown could be suffocating. When it came to everything he did, every decision he made, he had to first consider his title and how it would affect his standing with the people.

"My place is with my family," he told Vanessa. "It's what is expected of me."

Mia gurgled and swung her arms, vying for his attention, so he tickled her under the chin, which made her giggle.

"If I'd had to live with my dad all these years, I would be in a rubber room," Vanessa said, wearing a sour expression, which would seem to suggest animosity.

"You don't get along?"

"With my father, it's his way or the highway. Let's just say that he has a problem with decisions I've made."

"Which ones, if you don't mind my asking?"

She sighed. "Oh, pretty much all of them. It's kind of ironic if you think about it. There are people who dislike me because I'm too perfect, but in my dad's eyes I've never done a single thing right."

He couldn't help thinking that must have been an exaggeration. No parent could be that critical. "Surely he's pleased now that you're planning to marry a king."

"I could tell him I'm the new Mother Teresa and he'd find a way to write it off as a bad thing. Besides, I haven't told him. The only person who knows where I am is my best friend Jessy."

"Why keep it a secret?"

"I didn't want to say anything to anyone until I knew for sure that I really was going to marry Gabriel."

* * *

"What reason would you have not to marry him?" Marcus asked, and Vanessa hesitated. While she wanted to get to know Marcus better, she wasn't sure how she felt about discussing the private details of her relationship with his father. But at the same time, she hated to clam up now, as this outing was definitely going better than expected. And as she sat there on the rough wool blanket in the shade, the salty ocean air cooling her sunbaked skin, her daughter playing happily between them, she felt a deep sense of peace that she hadn't experienced in a very long time.

The first hour or so had been a bit like tiptoeing around in a minefield, her every move monitored, each word dissected for hidden meaning. But little by little she began to relax, and so did Marcus. The truth is, he was more like his father than she'd imagined. Sure, he was a bit intense at times, but he was very intelligent with a quick wit, and a wry sense of humor. And though it was obvious that he wasn't quite sure what to make of her—which wasn't unusual as she always seemed to fall somewhere outside of people's expectations—she had the feeling that maybe he was starting to like her. Or at the very least dislike her less. And he clearly adored Mia, who—the little flirt—hadn't taken her eyes off him for hours.

"Unless you'd rather not discuss it," Marcus said, his tone, and the glint of suspicion in his dark eyes, suggesting that she had something to hide.

She fidgeted with the corner of the blanket. Even though her relationship with Gabriel was none of his business, to not answer would look suspicious, but the truth might only validate his reservations about her. "My relationship with Gabriel is…complicated."

"How complicated could it be? You love him, don't you?"

There was a subtle accusation in his tone. Just when

she thought things were going really well, when she believed he was having a change of heart, he was back to the business of trying to discredit her, to expose her as a fraud. Well, maybe she should just give him what he wanted. It didn't seem as though it would make a difference at this point.

"I love him," she said. "I'm just not sure I'm *in* love with him."

"What's the difference?"

Did he honestly not know, or did he think she didn't? Or was he possibly just screwing with her? "Your father is an amazing human being. He's smart and he's kind and I respect him immensely. I love him as a friend, and I want him to be happy. I know that marrying me would make him happy, or at least he's told me it will. And of course I would love for Mia to have someone to call Daddy."

"But?" Marcus asked, leaning back on his arms, stretching his long legs out in front of him, as if he were settling in for a good story.

"But I want *me* to be happy, too. I deserve it."

"My father doesn't make you happy?"

"He does but…" She sighed. There was really no getting around this. "What are your feelings about intimacy before marriage?"

He didn't even hesitate. "It's immoral."

His answer took her aback. "Well, this is a first."

"What?"

"I've never met a twenty-eight-year-old virgin."

His brows slammed together. "I never said that I'm…"

He paused, realizing that he'd painted himself into a corner, and the look on his face was priceless.

"Oh, so what you're saying is, it's only immoral for your father to be intimate before marriage. For you it's fine?"

"My father is from a different generation. He thinks differently."

"Well, that's one thing you're right about. And it's a big part of my problem."

"What do you mean?"

"I believe two people should know whether or not they're sexually compatible before they jump into a marriage, because let's face it, sex is a very important part of a lasting relationship. Don't you agree?"

"I suppose it is."

"You suppose? Be honest. Would you marry a woman you'd never slept with?"

He hesitated, then said, "Probably not."

"Well, Gabriel is so traditional he won't even kiss me until we're officially engaged. And he considers sex before the wedding completely out of the question."

"You seriously want me to believe that you and my father have never…" He couldn't seem to make himself say the words, which she found kind of amusing.

"Is that really so surprising? You said yourself he's from a different generation. He didn't have sex with your mom until their wedding night, and even then he said it took a while to get all the gears moving smoothly."

Marcus winced.

"Sorry. TMI?"

"TMI?"

"Too much information?"

He nodded. "A bit."

"Honestly, I don't know why I'm telling you *any* of this, seeing as how it's really none of your business. And nothing I say is going to change the way you feel about me."

"So why are you telling me?"

"Maybe it's that I've gone through most of my life being

unfairly judged and I'm sick of it. I really shouldn't care if you like me or not, but for some stupid reason, I still do."

Marcus looked as if he wasn't sure what to believe. "I don't *dis*like you."

"But you don't trust me. Which is only fair, I guess, since I don't trust you either."

Seven

Instead of looking insulted, Marcus laughed, which completely confused Vanessa.

"You find that amusing?" she asked.

"What I find amusing is that you said it to my face. Do you ever have a thought that you *don't* express?"

"Sometimes." Like when she hadn't told him how his pale gray linen pants hugged his butt just right, and the white silk short sleeved shirt brought out the sun-bronzed tones of his skin. And she didn't mention how the dark shadow of stubble on his jaw made her want to reach up and touch his face. Or the curve of his mouth made her want to…well, never mind. "When I was a kid, every time I expressed an idea or a thought, my father shot it down. He had this way of making me feel inferior and stupid, and I'm *not* stupid. It just took a while to figure that out. And now I say what I feel, and I don't worry about what other people think, because most of them don't matter.

When it comes to my self-worth, the only opinion that really matters is my own. And though it took a long time to get here, I'm actually pretty happy with who I am. Sure, my life isn't perfect, and I still worry about making mistakes, but I know that I'm capable and smart, and if I do make a mistake, I'll learn from it."

"So what will you do?" he asked. "About my father, I mean. If he won't compromise his principles."

"I'm hoping that if we spend more time together, I'll just know that it's right."

"You said it yourself, you're a very beautiful woman, and my father seems to have very strong feelings for you. I'm quite certain that with little effort you could persuade him to compromise his principles."

Was he actually suggesting she *seduce* Gabriel? And why, when Marcus said she was beautiful, did it cause a little shiver of delight? She'd heard the same words so many times from so many men, they had lost their significance. Why was he so different? And why did she care *what* he thought of her?

And why on earth had she started this conversation in the first place?

"I would never do that," she told Marcus. "I respect him too much."

Mia began to fuss and Vanessa jumped on the opportunity to end this strange and frankly *inappropriate* chat. No matter what she did or said, or how she acted, the situation with Marcus just seemed to get weirder and weirder.

"I should get her back to the palace and down for a nap. And I could probably use one too." She was still on L.A. time, and despite being exhausted last night, she'd slept terribly.

He pushed himself to his feet. "Let's go."

Together they cleaned up the picnic, and to Vanessa's

surprise, Marcus lifted Mia up and held her while she folded the blanket. Even more surprising was how natural he appeared holding her, and how, when she reached to take her back, Mia clung to him and laid her head on his shoulder.

Little traitor, she thought, but she couldn't resist smiling. "I guess she wants you," she told Marcus, who looked as if he didn't mind at all.

They gathered the rest of their things and walked back to the limo waiting in the marina parking lot. They piled into the air-conditioned backseat, and she buckled Mia into her car seat. She expected that they would go straight back to the palace but instead, Marcus had the driver stop outside one of the shops they had visited earlier and went inside briefly. He came out several minutes later carrying a small bag that he slipped into his pants pocket before climbing back in the car, and though she was curious as to what was in it, she didn't ask, for fear of opening up yet another can of worms. He'd probably picked out a gift for his girlfriend. Because men who looked the way he did, and were filthy rich princes, always had a lady friend—if not two or three. And according to Gabriel, his son was never short on female companionship.

Mia fell asleep on the ride back, and when they pulled up to the front doors to the palace, before Vanessa had a chance, Marcus unhooked her from the car seat and plucked her out.

"I can carry her," she told him.

"I've got her," he said, and not only did he carry her all the way up to the nursery, he laid her in her crib and covered her up, the way a father would if Mia had one. And somewhere deep down a part of Vanessa ached for all the experiences her daughter had missed in her short life. Because she knew what it was like to lose a parent, to miss that connection. She hoped with all her heart that Gabriel could fill the void, that these months without a father hadn't left a permanent scar on Mia.

"She was really good today," he said, grinning down at Mia while she slept soundly.

"She's a pretty easygoing baby. You saw her at her very worst yesterday."

Vanessa let Karin know to listen for Mia so she could take a quick nap herself—thinking this nanny business was sort of nice after all—then Marcus walked her down the hall to her room. She stopped at the door and turned to him. "Thank you for taking me to the village today. I actually had a really good time."

One brow lifted a fraction. "And that surprises you?"

"Yeah, it does. I figured it could go either way."

The corners of his mouth crept up into a smile and those dimples dented his cheeks. Which made her heart go pitter-patter. He was too attractive for his own good. And hers.

"Too honest for you?" she asked him.

He shrugged. "I think I'm getting used to it."

Well, that was a start.

"My father would like me to take you to the history museum tomorrow," he said.

"Oh."

One brow rose. "Oh?"

"Well, I'm still pretty exhausted from the trip and I thought a day to just lie around by the pool might be nice. Mia loves playing in the water and I desperately need a tan. Back home I just never seem to have time to catch any sun. And you don't need to feel obligated to hang out with us. I'm sure you have things you need to do."

"You're sure?"

"I am."

"Then we can see the museum another day?"

She nodded. "That would be perfect."

He started to turn, then paused and said, "Oh, I almost forgot."

He pulled the bag from the shop out of his pocket and handed it to her. "This is for you."

Perplexed, she took it from him. "What is it?"

"Look and see."

She opened the bag and peered inside, her breath catching when she recognized the contents. "But…how did you know?"

"I saw you admiring them."

He didn't miss a thing, did he?

She pulled the earrings from the bag. They were hand-crafted with small emeralds set inside delicate silver swirls, and she'd fallen in love with them the instant she'd seen them in the shop, but at one hundred and fifty euros they had been way out of her budget.

"Marcus, they're lovely." She looked up at him. "I don't get it."

Hands hooked casually in his pants pockets, he shrugged. "If you had been there with my father, I don't doubt that he would have purchased them on the spot. It's what he would have wanted me to do."

She couldn't help but think that this meant something. Something significant. "I don't even know what to say. Thank you so much."

"What is it you Americans say? It's not a big deal?"

No, it was a *very* big deal.

It bothered her when Gabriel bought her things. It was as if he felt it necessary to buy her affections. But Marcus had no reason to buy her anything, other than the fact that he *wanted* to. It came from the heart. More so than any gift Gabriel had gotten her—or at least, that was the way she saw it.

Swallowing back tears of pure happiness—unsure of why it even mattered so much to her—she smiled and said, "I should go. Gabriel will be Skyping me soon."

"Of course. I'll see you tomorrow."

She watched him walk down the hall until he disappeared around the corner, then slipped into her room and shut the door behind her. Knowing how much it meant to Gabriel, she had really been hoping that she and Marcus could be friends. And now it seemed that particular wish might actually come true.

Marcus pushed off the edge of the pool for his final lap, his arms slicing through the water, heavy with fatigue due to the extra thirty minutes he'd spent in the pool pondering his earlier conversation with Vanessa. If what she said was true, and she and his father hadn't been intimate, what else could have possibly hooked him in? Her youth, and the promise of a fresh beginning, maybe?

Marcus's mother had confided once, a long time ago, that she and his father had hoped to have a large family, but due to complications from Marcus's birth—details she'd mercifully left out—more children became an impossibility. Maybe he saw this as his chance to start the family he always wanted but could never have. Because surely someone as adept at parenting as Vanessa would want more children.

Or maybe he saw what Marcus had seen today. A woman who was smart and funny and a little bizarre. And of course beautiful.

So much so that you had to buy her a present?

He reached the opposite end of the pool, debated stopping, then flipped over and pushed off one last time.

He really had no idea why he'd bought Vanessa the earrings. But as they were on their way back to the palace and he saw the shop, he heard himself asking the driver to stop, and before he knew what he was doing, he was inside, handing over his Visa card, and the clerk was bagging his purchase.

Maybe he and Vanessa had made some sort of...*connection*. But that wasn't even the point, because what he'd told her was true. If his father had seen her admiring the earrings he would have purchased them on the spot. Marcus did it to please his father and nothing more.

But the surprise on her face when she opened the bag and realized what was inside...

She looked so impressed and so grateful, he worried that she might burst into tears. That would have been really awful, because there was nothing worse than a woman in the throes of an emotional meltdown. And all for such a simple and inexpensive gift. If her only concern was wealth, wouldn't she have balked at anything but diamonds or precious gems? And if she were using his father, why would she admit that she wasn't in love with him? Why would she have discussed it at all?

Maybe, subconsciously, he'd seen it as some sort of test. One that she had passed with flying colors.

Marcus reached the opposite edge and hoisted himself up out of the water, slicking his hair back, annoyed that he was wasting any time debating this with himself.

He sighed and squinted at the sun, which hung close to the horizon, a reddish-orange globe against the darkening sky. The evening breeze cooled his wet skin. The fact of the matter was, though he didn't want to like Vanessa, he couldn't seem to help himself. He'd never met anyone quite like her.

From the table where he'd left it, his cell phone began to ring. Thinking it could be his father with an update about Aunt Trina, he pushed himself to his feet and grabbed the phone, but when he saw the number he cursed under his breath. He wasn't interested in anything his ex had to say, and after three weeks of avoiding her incessant phone calls and text messages, he would have expected that she'd gotten the point by now.

Apparently not. Leaving him to wonder what it was he'd seen in her in the first place. How could someone who had bewitched him so thoroughly now annoy him so completely?

Aggressive women had never really been Marcus's first choice in a potential mate. But sexy, sultry and with a body to die for, Carmela had pursued him with a determination that put other women to shame. She was everything he could have wanted in a wife, or so he believed, and because she came from a family of considerable wealth and power, he never once worried that she was after his money. Six months in he'd begun to think about engagement rings and wedding arrangements, only to discover that he'd been terribly wrong about her. And though the first week after the split had been difficult, he'd gradually begun to realize his feelings for her were based more on infatuation and lust than real love. His only explanation was that he'd been emotionally compromised by his mother's death. And the fact that she had taken advantage of that was, in his opinion, despicable. And unforgivable.

He shuddered to think what would have happened had he actually proposed, or God forbid *married* her. And he was disappointed in himself that he'd let it go as far as he had, that he'd been so blinded by her sexual prowess. And honestly, the actual sex wasn't that great. Physically, she gave him everything he could ask for and more, but emotionally their encounters had left him feeling…empty. Maybe it had been an unconscious need for a deeper connection that had kept him coming back for more, but now, looking back, he could hardly believe what a fool he'd been.

His text message alert chimed, and of course it was from her.

"Enough already," he ground out, turning on his heel and flinging his cell phone into the pool. Only when he looked up past the pool to the garden path did he realize that he had an audience.

Vanessa stood on the garden path watching Marcus's cell phone hit the surface of the water, then slowly sink down, until it was nothing but a murky shadow against the tile bottom.

"You know," she told Marcus, who clearly hadn't realized that she was standing there, "I have that same impulse nearly every day of my life. Although I usually imagine tossing it off the roof of the hotel, or under the wheels of a passing semi."

He sighed and raked a hand through his wet hair, the last remnants of evening sunshine casting a warm glow over his muscular arms and chest, his toned to perfection thighs. And though the Speedo covered the essentials, it was wet and clingy and awfully...well, revealing.

Ugh, what was she, *twelve?* It wasn't as if she hadn't seen a mostly naked man before. Or a completely naked one for that matter. Of course, none of them had been quite so...yummy.

Remember, this is your almost fiancé's son you're ogling. The thought filled her with guilt. Okay, maybe that was an exaggeration, but she did feel a mild twinge.

"That was childish of me," he said, looking as if he were disappointed in himself.

"But did it feel good?" she asked.

He hesitated, then a smile tilted the corners of his mouth. "Yeah, it did. And I needed a new one anyway."

"Then it's worth it."

"What are you doing out here?" He grabbed his towel from the table and began to dry himself. His arms, his pecs, the wall of his chest…

Oh boy. What she wouldn't give to be that towel right now.

Think son-in-law, Vanessa.

"Mia went down early, and I was feeling a little restless," she told him. "I thought I would take a walk."

"After all the walking we did today? You should be exhausted."

"I'm on my feet all day every day. Today was a cakewalk. Plus I'm trying to acclimate myself to the time change. If I go to bed too early I'll never adjust. And for the record, I am exhausted. I haven't slept well since I got here."

"Why not?" He draped the towel over the back of a chair, then took a seat, leaning casually back, with not a hint of shame. Not that he had anything to be ashamed of, and there was nothing more appealing than a man so comfortable in his own skin. Especially one who looked as good as he did.

"I keep waking up and listening for Mia, then I remember that she's down the hall. And of course I feel compelled to get up and go check on her. Then it's hard to get back to sleep. I thought a walk might relax me."

"Why don't you join me for a drink?" he said. "It might take the edge off."

She'd never been one to drink very often, and lately, with an infant in her care, she'd more or less stopped altogether. But now there was a nanny to take over if Vanessa needed her. Maybe it would be okay, just this once, to let her hair down a little.

And maybe Marcus would put some clothes on.

"Yeah, sure. I'd love one," she told him, and as if by magic, or probably ESP, the butler materialized from a set of French doors that led to…well, honestly, she wasn't sure where they led. She had gone out a side door to the garden, one patrolled by armed guards. She probably wouldn't have been able to find even that if Camille hadn't shown her the way. The palace had more twists and turns than a carnival fun house.

"What would you like?" Marcus asked.

"What do you have?"

"We have a fully stocked bar. George can make anything you desire."

She summoned a list of drinks that she used to enjoy, and told George, "How about…a vodka tonic with a twist of lime?"

George nodded, turned to Marcus, and in a voice as craggy and old as the man said, "Your highness?"

"The same for me. And could you please let Cleo know that I'll be needing a new phone, and a new number."

George nodded and limped off, looking as if every step took a great deal of effort.

Vanessa took a seat across from Marcus and when George was out of earshot asked, "How old is he?"

"I'm really not sure. Eighties, nineties. All I know is that he's been with the family since my father was a child."

"He looks as if he has a hard time getting around."

"He has rheumatoid arthritis. And though his staff does most of the real work these days, I assure you he's still quite capable, and has no desire to retire anytime soon. Honestly, I don't think he has anywhere else to go. As far as I'm aware, he's never been married. He has no children. We're his only family."

"That's kind of sad," Vanessa said, feeling a sudden burst of sympathy for the cranky old butler. She couldn't imagine being so alone in the world. Or maybe he didn't see it that way. Maybe his career, his attachments with the royal family and the other staff, were all the fulfillment he needed.

"If you'll excuse me a moment," Marcus said, rising from his seat. "I should probably go change before I catch a chill."

She had wanted him to put clothes on, but she couldn't deny being slightly disappointed. But the blistering heat of the afternoon did seem to be evaporating with the setting sun, and a cool breeze had taken its place.

While he was gone, Vanessa slipped her sandals off and walked over to the pool. She sat on the edge, dipping her feet in water warm enough to bathe in. She'd never been much of a swimmer—or into any sort of exercise, despite how many times her father had pushed her to try different sports and activities. She had the athletic prowess of a brick, and about as much grace. And firearms being his passion, he'd tried relentlessly to get her on the firing range. He'd gone as far as to get her a hunting rifle for her fourteenth birthday, but guns scared her half to death and she'd refused to even touch it. She'd often entertained the idea that he would have been much happier with a son, and had someone offered a trade, he'd have jumped at the chance.

As the last vestiges of daylight dissolved into the horizon and the garden and pool lights switched on, Vanessa noticed the shadow of Marcus's cell phone, wondering what—or *who*—had driven him to chuck it into the water. From what Gabriel had told her, Marcus was even-tempered and composed, so whatever it was must have really upset him.

She sighed, wondering what Gabriel was doing just then. Probably sitting at the hospital, where he spent the majority of his day. Trina was still very sick, but responding to the treatment, and the doctors were cautiously optimistic that she would make a full recovery. Though Vanessa felt selfish for even thinking it, she hoped that meant Gabriel would be home soon. She wanted to get her life back on track and plan her future, because at the moment she'd never felt more unsettled or restless. And it wasn't fair to Mia to keep her living in limbo, although to be honest she seemed no worse for wear.

"Your drink," Marcus said, and the sound of his voice made her jump.

She turned to find him dressed in khaki shorts and a pale silk, short sleeved shirt, that could have been gray or light blue. It was difficult to tell in the muted light.

"Sorry, didn't mean to startle you." He handed her one of the two glasses he was holding and sat next to her on the edge, slipping his bare feet into the water beside hers. He was so close, she could smell chlorine on his skin, and if she were to move her leg just an inch to the right, her thigh would touch his. For some reason the idea of actually doing it made her heart beat faster. Not that she ever would.

Eight

"I guess I was lost in thought," she said. "When I talked to Gabriel today he said that your aunt is responding to the treatment."

Marcus nodded, sipping his drink, then setting it on the tile beside him. "I spoke with him this afternoon. He said they're optimistic."

"I was kind of hoping that meant he would be home sooner. Which is pretty thoughtless, I know." She took a swallow of her drink and her eyes nearly crossed as it slid down her throat, instantly warming her insides. "Wow! That's strong."

"Would you care for something different?"

"No, I like it." She took another sip, but a smaller one this time. "It has kick, but the vodka is very…I don't know, smooth, I guess."

"George only stocks the best. And for the record, you're not thoughtless. I would say that you've been tremendously patient given the circumstances. Had it been me, considering my less than warm greeting, I probably would have turned around and gotten back on the plane."

"If it hadn't been for Mia, I might have. But another thirteen hours in the air would have done me in for sure."

Marcus was quiet for a minute, gazing at the water and the ripples their feet made on the surface. Then he mumbled something that sounded like a curse and shook his head.

"Is something wrong?" she asked him.

"Your proclivity toward brutal honesty must be rubbing off on me."

"What do you mean?"

"I probably shouldn't tell you this, and I would be breaking a confidence in doing so, but I feel as if you deserve the truth."

Vanessa's heart sank a little. "Why do I get the feeling I'm not going to like this?"

"My father told me that he would likely be three or four weeks. He didn't want you to know for fear that you wouldn't stay. It's why he wanted me to keep you entertained."

Her heart bottomed out. "But my visit will only be for six weeks. Which will leave us only two or three to get to know one another better."

What if that wasn't enough time?

Marcus shrugged. "So you'll stay longer."

Feeling hurt and betrayed, her nerves back on edge, Vanessa took another swallow of her drink. If Gabriel lied about this, what else was he lying about? "I can't stay longer. My leave from work is only six weeks. If I don't go back I'll get fired. Until I know for sure whether I'm staying here, I need that job. Otherwise I would have nothing to go back for. I have very little savings. Mia and I would essentially be on the streets."

"My father is a noble man," Marcus said. "Even if you decided not to marry him, he would never allow that to happen. He would see that you were taken care of."

"If he's so noble why would he lie to me in the first place?"

"He only did it because he cares for you."

It was a moot point because she would never take his charity. And even if she would, there was no guarantee that Gabriel would be so generous.

Marcus must have read her mind, because he added, "If he didn't see that you were taken care of, *I* would."

His words stunned her. "Why? As of this afternoon, you still believed that I'm using him."

"I guess you could say that I've had a change of heart."

"But, *why?*"

His laugh was rich and warm and seemed to come from deep within him. "You perplex me, Vanessa. You tell me that I should give you a chance, but when I do, you question my motives. Perhaps it's you who needs to give *me* a chance."

She had indeed said that. "You're right. I guess I'm just feeling very out of sorts right now." She touched his arm lightly, found it to be warm and solid under her palm. "I'm sorry."

He looked at her hand resting on his forearm, then up into her eyes, and said, "Apology accepted."

There was something in their sooty depths, some emotion that made her heart flip in her chest, and suddenly she felt warm all over.

It's just the vodka, she assured herself, easing her hand away and taking a deep swallow from her glass.

"Would you care for another?" Marcus asked.

She looked down and realized that her glass was empty, while his was still more than half full.

"I probably shouldn't," she said, feeling her muscles slacken with the warm glow of inebriation. It was the most relaxed she had felt in weeks. Would one more drink be such a bad thing? In light of what she'd just learned, didn't she deserve it? With Mia in the care of her nanny, what reason did Vanessa have to stop? "But what the hell, why not? It's not as if I have to drive home, right?"

Marcus gestured randomly and George must have been watching for it—which to her was slightly creepy—because moments later he appeared with a fresh drink. And either this one wasn't as strong, or the first had numbed her to the intensity of the vodka. Whatever the reason, she drank liberally.

"So, would I be overstepping my bounds to ask why you drowned your phone?" Vanessa said.

"A persistent ex-lover."

"I take it you dumped her."

"Yes, but only after I caught her in the backseat of the limo with my best friend."

"Ouch. Were they…you know…"

"Yes. Quite enthusiastically."

She winced. So he'd lost his mother, his girlfriend and his best friend. How sucky was that? "I'm sorry."

He slowly kicked his feet back and forth through the water, the side of his left foot brushing against her right one. She had to force herself not to jump in surprise.

"Each tried to pin it on the other. She's still trying to convince me that he lured her there under false pretenses, and once he had her in the car he more or less attacked her."

She let her foot drift slightly to the left, to see if it would happen again. "She cried rape?"

"More or less."

"What did your friend say?"

"That she lured him into the car, and she made the first move."

"Who do you believe?"

"Neither of them. In the thirty seconds or so that I was standing there in shock, she never once told him no, and she wasn't making any attempt to stop him. I think all the moaning they were both doing spoke for itself."

His foot bumped hers again, and a tiny thrill shot up from her foot and through her leg, settling in places that were completely inappropriate considering their relationship.

"Were you in love with her?" Vanessa asked him.

"I thought I was, but I realize now it was just lust."

"Sometimes it's hard to tell the two apart."

"Is that how it is with you and my father?"

What she felt for Gabriel was definitely not lust. "Not at all. Gabriel is a good friend, and I love and respect him for that. It's the lust part we need to work on."

Her candor seemed to surprise him. "And he knows you feel that way?"

"I've been completely honest with him. He's convinced that my feelings for him will grow. And I'm hoping he's right."

His foot brushed hers again, and this time she could swear it was intentional. Was he honestly playing footsies with her? And why was her heart beating so fast, her skin tingling with awareness? And why was she mentally willing him to touch her in other places too, but with his hands?

Because there is something seriously wrong with you, honey. But knowing that didn't stop her from leaning back on her arms and casually shifting her leg so her thigh brushed his.

Now this, what she was feeling right now, *this* was lust. And it was so wrong.

"I learned last week that her father's company is in financial crisis and on the verge of collapse," Marcus said, and it took Vanessa a second to realize that he was talking about his ex. "I guess she thought that an alliance with the royal family would have pulled him from the inevitable depths of bankruptcy."

"So you think she was using you?"

"It seems a safe assumption."

Well, that at least explained why he was so distrustful of Vanessa. He obviously looked at her and saw his ex. She shook her head in disgust and said, "What a bitch."

Marcus's eyes widened, and Vanessa slapped a hand across her mouth. Why couldn't she learn to hold her tongue? "Sorry, that was totally inappropriate of me."

Instead of looking angry, or put out, Marcus just laughed.

"No, it was more appropriate than you would imagine. And unfortunately she wasn't the first. But usually I'm better at spotting it. I think my mother's death left such a gaping hole, and I was so desperate to fill it I had blinders on."

"You want to hear something ironic? In my junior year of high school, I caught my boyfriend in the back of his car with my so-called friend."

His brow lifted. "Was it a limo?"

She laughed. "Hardly. It was piece of crap SUV."

"What did you do when you caught them?"

"Threw a brick through the back window."

He laughed. "Maybe that's what I should have done."

"I was really mad. I had just written his history term paper for him, and he got an A. I found out later from one of my 'friends' that he'd only dated me because I was smart, and in most of the same classes and willing to help him with his homework. I was stupid enough to do it for him. And let him copy off my tests. He played football, and if his grades dropped he would be kicked off the team. Pretty much everyone knew he was using me."

"And no one told you?"

"Suffice it to say they weren't my friends after that. My dad was reassigned a month later. It was one of the few times I was really relieved to be starting over."

"I hope you at least reported him to the headmaster," Marcus said.

"You have no idea how badly I wanted to go to our teachers and the principal and tell them what I'd been doing, that his work was really my work. Not only could I have gotten him kicked off the team, he would have been expelled."

"Why didn't you?"

"Because I would have been expelled too. And my father would have *killed* me. Not to mention that it was completely embarrassing. I should have known, with his reputation, he would never seriously date a girl who didn't put out unless he was after something else. Not that he didn't try to get in my pants every chance he got."

"You shouldn't blame yourself. You have a trusting nature. That's a good thing."

Not always. "Unfortunately, I seem to attract untrustworthy men. It's as if I have the word *gullible* stamped in invisible ink on my forehead, and only jerks can see it."

"Not all men use women."

"All the men I've known do."

"Surely not everyone has been that bad."

"Trust me, if there was a record for the world's worst luck with men, I would hold it. When Mia's dad walked out on me, I swore I would never let a man use me again. That I would never trust so blindly. But then I met Gabriel and he's just so…wonderful. And he treated me as if I were something special."

"That's because he thinks you are. From the minute he returned home he couldn't stop talking about you." He laid a hand on her arm, gave it a gentle squeeze, his dark eyes soft with compassion. "He's not using you, Vanessa."

Weird, but yesterday he was convinced she was using his father. When had everything gotten so turned around?

And why, as they had a heart-to-heart talk about his father—one that should have drawn her closer to Gabriel—could she only think about Marcus? Why did she keep imagining what it would be like to lay her hand on his muscular thigh, feel the crisp dark hair against her palm? Why did she keep looking at his mouth, and wondering how it would feel pressed against hers?

Maybe they both would have been better off if he kept acting like a jerk, because it was becoming painfully clear that Vanessa had developed a major crush. On the wrong man.

"Do you think someone can fall in love, real love, in a matter of two weeks?" Vanessa asked Marcus.

He could tell her that he believed falling in love so fast was nothing but a fairy tale, and that he thought his father was rebounding. What he felt for Vanessa was infatuation and nothing more, and he would realize that when he returned from Italy. Marcus knew if he told Vanessa that, she was confused and vulnerable enough that she might actually believe him. Which would discourage her, and fill her with self-doubt, and might ultimately make her leave. And wasn't that what he'd wanted?

But now, he couldn't make himself say the words.

Something had changed. He was instead telling her things that would make her want to stay, and for reasons that had nothing to do with his father's happiness, and everything to do with Marcus's fascination with her. She wasn't helping matters by encouraging him, by moving closer when he touched her, looking up at him with those expressive blue eyes. And did she have to smell so good? Most of the women he knew bathed themselves in cloying perfume, Carmela included, but Vanessa smelled of soap and shampoo. And he could smell that only because they were sitting so close to one another. *Too* close. If he had any hope of fighting these inappropriate feelings, he really needed to back off.

"I believe that when it comes to love, anything is possible," he told her, which wasn't a lie exactly. He just didn't believe it in this case. And the idea that she might be hurt again disturbed him more than he could have ever imagined possible. Maybe because he knew it was inevitable. He just hoped that when his father let her down, he did it gently. Or maybe after waiting for his father for so many weeks, she would grow frustrated and decide she didn't want to stay after all.

Now that Marcus had gotten to know her better, he wasn't any more sure of what to expect. He'd never met a woman more confusing or unpredictable. Yet in a strange way, he felt he could relate to her—understand her even— which made no sense at all.

But what baffled him most was how wrong he'd been about her, when he was so sure he'd had her pegged. He hadn't given his father nearly enough credit, had just assumed he was too vulnerable to make intelligent choices, and for that Marcus would always feel foolish.

George appeared at his side with two fresh drinks. Marcus took them and held one out to Vanessa. She looked in the glass she was still holding as if she were surprised to realize that it was empty.

"Oh, I really shouldn't," she said, but as he moved to give it back to George, added, "But it would be a shame to let the good stuff go to waste. No more after this though."

George shuffled off with their empty glasses, shaking his head in either amusement or exasperation, Marcus couldn't be sure which. None of the staff were sure what to think of her, and that was in large part Marcus's fault, as he'd made his feelings about her visit quite clear from the moment his father had broken the news. Now he knew that he'd unfairly judged her, and that was something he needed to rectify.

"Your dad said that when he met your mom it was love at first sight," she said. "And it was a big scandal because she wasn't a royal."

"Yes, my grandparents were very traditional. There was already a marriage arranged for him but he loved my mother. They threatened to disown him. He said it was the only time in his life that he rebelled against their wishes."

"That must have been difficult for your mom. To know that they hated her so much they would disown their own child."

"It wasn't her so much as the idea of her that they resented, but things improved after I was born. My father was an only child, so they were happy that she'd given my father a male heir."

"So your father wouldn't mind if you married a non-royal?"

"My parents have been very insistent my entire life that as sole heir it's imperative I also produce an heir, but they want me to marry for love."

"Like they did."

He nodded.

"What was your mom like?" she asked.

Just thinking of her brought a smile to his face. "Beautiful, loyal, outspoken—more so than some people thought a queen should be. She grew up in a middle-class family in Italy, so she had a deep respect for the common man. You actually remind me of her in a way."

She blinked in surprise. "*I* do?"

"She was brave and smart, and she wasn't afraid to speak her mind. Even if it got her into trouble sometimes. And she was a positive role model to young women."

"Brave?" she said, looking at him as though he'd completely lost his mind. "I'm constantly terrified that I'm doing the wrong thing, or making the wrong choice."

"But that doesn't stop you from *making* the choice, and that takes courage."

"Maybe, but I fail to see how I'm a role model to women. My life has been one bad move after another."

How could she not see it, not be proud of her accomplishments? "You're well traveled, intelligent, successful. You're an excellent mother, raising a child with no help. What young woman wouldn't look up to you?"

She bit her lip, and for a second he thought she might start crying. "That's probably the nicest thing anyone has ever said to me. Though I'm pretty sure that I don't deserve it. I'm a gigantic walking disaster waiting to happen."

"That's your father talking," he said.

"In part. But I can't deny that I've made some really dumb decisions in my life."

"Everybody does. How will you learn if you don't make occasional mistakes?"

"The problem is, I don't seem to be learning from mine."

Why couldn't she see what he did? Was she really so beaten down by her father's overinflated ideals that she had no self-confidence left? And what could he do to make her believe otherwise? How could he make her see how gifted and special and unique she really was? "You don't give yourself enough credit. If you weren't an extraordinary person, do you really think my father would have fallen so hard for you so fast?"

Nine

Their eyes met and Vanessa's were so filled with hope and vulnerability, Marcus had to resist the urge to pull her into his arms and hold her. His gaze dropped to her mouth, and her lips looked so plump and soft, he couldn't help but wonder how they would feel, how they would taste.

The sudden pull of lust in his groin caught him completely off guard, but he couldn't seem to look away.

Carmela and most other women he'd dated favored fitted, low-cut blouses and skintight jeans. They dressed to draw attention. In shorts and a T-shirt and with no makeup on her face, her pale hair cascading down in loose waves across her shoulders, Vanessa didn't look particularly sexy. Other than being exceptionally beautiful, she looked quite ordinary, yet he couldn't seem to keep his eyes off her.

Vanessa was the one to turn her head, but not before he saw a flash of guilt in her eyes, and he knew, whatever these improper feeling were, she was having them too.

Vanessa rubbed her arms. "It's getting chilly, huh?"

"Would you like to go inside?" he asked.

She shook her head, gazing up at the night sky. "Not yet."

"I could have George bring us something warm to drink."

"No, thank you."

They were both quiet for several minutes, but there was a question that had been nagging him since their conversation this afternoon in the park. "You said that you were afraid two or three weeks wouldn't be long enough to get to know my father better. I'm wondering, what guarantee did you have that four weeks would be? Or six?"

She shrugged. "There was no guarantee. But I had to at least try. For him. And for Mia."

"What about you?"

"For me, too," she said, avoiding his gaze.

Why did he get the feeling her own needs were pretty low on the priority scale? The way he saw it, either you were physically attracted to someone or you weren't. There was no gray area. And it seemed a bit selfish of his father to push her into something she clearly was unsure about.

She took a swallow of her drink, then blinked rapidly, setting her glass on the tile beside her. "You know, I think I've had enough. I feel a little woozy. And it's getting late. I should check on Mia."

It was odd, but although he'd had no intention of spending the evening with her, now he wasn't ready for it to end. All the more reason that it should. "Shall I walk you back to your room?"

"You might have to. I'm honestly not sure I could find it by myself."

"Tomorrow I'll have Cleo print a map for you." Two days ago it wouldn't have mattered to him, now he wanted her to feel comfortable in the palace. It was the least he could do.

He set his drink down and pulled himself to his feet, the night air cool against his wet skin, and extended a hand to help her. It felt so small and fragile, and it was a good thing he was holding on, because as he pulled her to her feet, she was so off balance she probably would have fallen into the pool.

"Are you okay?" he asked, pulling her away from the edge.

"Yeah." She blinked several times then gave her head a shake, as if to clear it, clutching his hand in a death grip. "Maybe I shouldn't have had that last drink."

"Would you like to sit back down?"

She took several seconds to get her bearings, then said, "I think I should probably just get to bed."

His first thought, depraved as it was, was "Why don't I join you." But, while he could think it, and perhaps even wish it a little, it was something he would never say out loud. And even more important, never do.

Could this be more embarrassing?

Feeling like an idiot, Vanessa clung to Marcus's arm as he led her across the patio. So much for letting her hair down a little.

"On top of everything else, now you probably think I have a drinking problem," she said.

Marcus grinned, his dimples forming dents in both cheeks, and she felt that delicious little zing. Did he have to be so...*adorable?*

"Maybe if you'd had ten drinks," he said, stopping by the table so she could grab her phone and they could both slip into their sandals. "But you only had three, and you didn't even finish the last one. I'm betting it has more to do with the jet lag."

"Jet lag can do that?"

"Sure. So can fatigue. Are you certain you can make it upstairs? I could carry you."

Yeah, because that wouldn't be completely humiliating. Besides, she liked holding on to his arm. And she couldn't help wondering what it would be like to touch him in other places. Not that she would ever try. She probably wouldn't be feeling this way at all if it weren't for the alcohol.

Well, okay, she probably would, but never in a million years would she act on it. Even though he thought she was smart and brave and successful. Plus, he'd left out beautiful. That was usually the first, and sometimes the only thing, that people noticed about her. Gabriel must have told her a million times. Remarkably, Marcus seemed to see past that.

"I think I can manage," she told him.

Clutching her cell phone in one hand and his forearm in the other, she wobbled slightly as he led her across the patio, but as they reached the French doors, she stopped. "Could we possibly walk around the side, through the garden?"

"What for?"

She chewed her lip, feeling like an irresponsible adolescent, which is probably how everyone else in the palace would see her as well. "I'm too embarrassed to have anyone see me this way. The entire staff already thinks I'm a horrible person. Now they're going to think I'm a lush, too."

"What does it matter what they think?"

"Please," she said, tugging him toward the garden path. "I feel so stupid."

"You shouldn't. But if it means that much to you, we'll go in the side entrance."

"Thank you."

Actually, now that she was on her feet, she felt steadier, but she kept holding on to his arm anyway. Just in case. Or just because it felt nice. He was tall and sturdy and reliable. And warm. He made her feel safe. She tried to recall if any man had made her feel that way before and drew a blank. Surely there must have been someone.

They headed down the path, around the back of the palace to the east side. At least, she was pretty sure it was east, or maybe it was west. Or north. Suddenly she felt all turned around. But whichever way it was, she remembered it from earlier, even though it was a lot darker now, despite the solar lights lining the path.

They were halfway around the building when Vanessa heard a sound on the flagstones behind them and wondered fleetingly if they were being followed. Being an L.A. resident, her first instinct was to immediately whip out her phone in case she needed to dial 911, which was how she realized her cell phone was no longer in her hand. The noise must have been her phone falling onto the path.

She let go of Marcus's arm and stopped, squinting to see in the dim light.

"What's wrong," he asked. "Are you going to be sick?"

She huffed indignantly. "I'm not *that* drunk. I dropped my phone."

"Where?"

"A few feet back, I think. I heard it hit the ground."

They backtracked, scouring the ground for several minutes, but it wasn't on or even near the path.

"Maybe it bounced into the flower bed," she said, crouching down to peer into the dense foliage, nearly falling on her butt in the process.

Marcus shook his head, looking grim. "If it did, we'll never find it at night."

"Call it!" Vanessa said, feeling rather impressed with herself for having such a brilliant idea in her compromised condition. "When we hear it ring, we'll know where it is."

"Right," he said hooking a thumb in the direction of the pool. "I'll go fish my phone out of the water and do that."

"Oh yeah, I forgot about that. Can't you borrow one?"

"Or we could look for your phone tomorrow."

"No!" Maybe he could blithely toss his electronic equipment away, but she worked for a living. Nor did she have a secretary to keep track of her life. "Besides the fact that it cost me a fortune, that phone is my life. It has my schedule and all my contacts and my music. What if it rains, or an animal gets it or something?"

He sighed loudly. "Wait here and I'll go get a phone."

She frowned. "By myself, in the dark?"

"I assure you the grounds are highly guarded and completely safe."

"What about that certain criminal element who would love to ransom the future queen?"

He smiled sheepishly. "Maybe that was a slight exaggeration. You'll be fine."

She'd expected as much. He'd been trying to drive her away, to make her *want* to leave. And as much as it annoyed her, she couldn't hold it against him. Not after all the nice things he'd said about her. Which she supposed was a big part of her problem. Someone said something nice about her and she went all gooey.

"You should stay in the general vicinity of where you lost it," Marcus warned her. "Or this could take all night."

"I'll stay right here," she said, flopping down on the path cross-legged to wait, the flagstone still warm from the afternoon sun.

Marcus grinned and shook his head. She watched as he backtracked from where they'd come, until he disappeared around a line of shrubs.

She sat there very still, listening to sounds of the night—crickets chirping and a mild breeze rustling the trees. And she swore, if she listened really hard, she could hear the faint hiss of the ocean, that if she breathed deep enough, she could smell the salty air. Or maybe it was just her imagination. Of all the different places her father had been stationed over the years, her favorite bases had been the ones near the water. And while she loved living close to the sea, the coast of California was exorbitantly expensive. Maybe someday. Maybe even here. The palace wasn't right on the water, but it was pretty darn close.

After a few minutes of waiting, her butt started to get sore, so she scooted off the flagstone path into the cool, prickly grass. Falling backward onto the spongy sod, she looked up at the sky. It was a crystal-clear night with a half moon, and even with the lights around the grounds, she could see about a million stars. In L.A. the only way to see the stars was to drive up to the mountains. She and Mia's dad used to do that. They would camp out in the bed of his truck, alternating between making love and watching the stars. She couldn't be sure, but she suspected that Mia may have actually been conceived in the bed of that truck. An unusual place to get pregnant, but nothing about her relationship with Paul had been typical. She used to think that was a good thing, and one of their strengths, because God knew those "normal" relationships she'd had were all a disaster. Until she came home to find a "Dear Vanessa" letter and realized she was wrong. Again. He hadn't even had the guts to tell her to her face that he wasn't ready for the responsibility of a child, and they were both better off without him.

So normal was bad, and eccentric was bad, which didn't leave much else. But royal, that was one she'd never tried, and never expected to have a chance to. Yet here she was. Lying on the palace lawn on a cool summer night under a sky cloaked with stars.

Which she had to admit wasn't very royal of her. She wondered if Gabriel's wife, or even Gabriel, had ever sprawled out on the grass and gazed up at the sky. Or skipped in the rain, catching drops on their tongues. Or snowflakes. Had Gabriel and Marcus ever bundled up and built a snowman together? Had they given it coal eyes and a carrot nose? Had they made snow angels or had snowball fights? And would she really be happy married to someone who didn't know how to relax and have fun, do something silly? Would Mia miss out on an important part of her childhood? Because *everyone* had to be silly every now and then.

Or was she worrying for nothing? Suffering from a typical case of insecurity? Was she creating problems where none really existed? Was she trying to sabotage a good thing because she was too afraid to take a chance?

So much for her being brave, huh?

She pondered that for a while, until she heard footsteps on the path, and glanced over to see Marcus walking toward her, looking puzzled. He stopped beside her, hands on his slim hips, and looked down. "You okay?"

She smiled and nodded. "It's a beautiful night. I'm looking at the stars."

He looked up at the sky, then back down at her. "Are you sure you didn't fall down?"

She swatted at him, but he darted out of the way, grinning.

"Could you join me?" she said. "Unless you're not allowed."

"Why wouldn't I be?"

"I thought maybe it wasn't royal enough."

"You know, you're not making a whole lot of sense."

"Do I ever?"

He laughed. "Good point."

And that apparently didn't matter, because he lay down beside her in the grass, so close their arms were touching. And she liked the way it felt. *A lot.* She liked being close to him, liked the warm fuzzy feeling coupled with that zing of awareness, and that urge to reach over and lace her fingers through his. It was exciting, and scary.

But of course she wouldn't do it, because even she wasn't that brave.

"You're right," he said, gazing up at the sky. "It is beautiful."

She looked over at him. "You think I'm weird, don't you."

"Not weird, exactly, but I can safely say that I've never met anyone like you."

"I don't know if I'm royalty material. I don't think I could give this up."

"Lying in the grass?"

She nodded.

"Who said you have to?"

"I guess I just don't know what's acceptable, and what isn't. I mean, if I marry Gabriel can I still build snowmen?"

"I don't see why not."

"Can I catch rain and snowflakes on my tongue?"

"You could try, I suppose."

"Can I walk in the sand in my bare feet, and make mud pies with Mia?"

"You know, we royals aren't so stuffy and uptight that we don't know how to have fun. We're just people. We lead relatively normal lives outside of the public eye."

But normal for him, and normal for her, were two very different things. "This all happened so abruptly. I guess I just don't know what to expect."

Marcus looked over at her. "You know that if you marry my father, you'll still be the same person you are right now. There's no magic potion or incantation that suddenly makes you royal. And there are no set rules." He paused then added, "Okay, I guess there are some rules. Certain protocol we have to follow. But you'll learn."

And Gabriel should have been the one explaining that to her, not Marcus. It was Gabriel she should have been getting to know, Gabriel she needed to bond with. Instead she was bonding with Marcus, and in a big way. She could feel it. She was comfortable with him, felt as if she could really be herself. Maybe because she wasn't worried about impressing him. Or maybe she was connecting in a small way. The truth was, everything had gotten so jumbled and confused, she wasn't sure how she felt about anything right now. And she was sure the drinks weren't helping.

Everything will be clearer tomorrow, she told herself. She would talk to Gabriel again, and remember how much she cared about him and missed him, and everything would go back to normal. She and Marcus would be friends, and she would stop having these irrational feelings.

"I've been thinking," Marcus said. "You should call your father and tell him where you are."

His suggestion—the fact that he'd even thought it— puzzled her. "So he can tell me that I'm making another stupid mistake? Why would I do that?"

"*Are* you making a mistake?"

If only she could answer that question, if she could hop a time machine and flash forward a year or so in the future, she would know how this would all play out. But that would be too easy. "I guess I won't know for sure until things go south."

He exhaled an exasperated sigh. "Okay, do you *think* you're making a mistake? Would you be here if you were sure this was going to end in disaster?"

She considered that, then said, "No, *I* don't think I'm making a mistake, because even if it doesn't work out, I got to visit a country I've never been to, and meet new people and experience new things. I got to stay in a palace and meet a prince. Even if he was kind of a doofus at first."

He smiled. "Then it doesn't matter what your father thinks. And I think that keeping this from him only makes it seem as though you have something to hide. If you really want him to respect you, and have confidence in your decisions, you've got to have faith in yourself first."

"Wow. That was incredibly insightful." And he was right. "You're speaking from experience, I assume."

"I'm the future leader of this country. It's vital I convey to the citizens that I'm confident in my abilities. It's the only way they'll trust me to lead them."

"Are you confident in your abilities?"

"Most of the time. There are days when the thought of that much responsibility scares the hell out of me. But part of being an effective leader means learning to delegate." He looked at her and grinned. "And always having someone else to pin the blame on when you screw up."

He was obviously joking, and his smile was such an adorable one, it made her want to reach out and touch his cheek. "You know, you have a really nice smile. You should do it more often."

He looked up at the stars. "I think this is probably the most I've smiled since we lost my mother."

"Really?"

"Life has been pretty dull since she died. She made everything fun and interesting. I guess that's another way that you remind me of her."

The warm fuzzy feeling his words gave her were swiftly replaced by an unsettling thought. If she was so much like Marcus's mom, could that be the reason Gabriel was so drawn to her? Did he see her as some sort of replacement for the original?

Second best?

That was silly. Of course he didn't.

And if it was so silly, why did she have a sudden sick, hollow feeling in the pit of her stomach?

Ten

Remember what you told Marcus, Vanessa reminded herself. *Even if this doesn't work out, it's not a mistake.* The thought actually made her feel a tiny bit better.

"Oh, by the way…" Marcus pulled a cell phone from his shorts pocket. "What's your number?"

She'd actually forgotten all about her phone. She told him the number and he dialed, and she felt it begin to rumble…in the front pocket of her shorts! "What the—"

She pulled it out, staring dumbfounded, and Marcus started to laugh. "But…I heard it fall."

"Whatever you heard, it obviously wasn't your phone."

"Oh, geez. I'm sorry."

"It's okay." He pushed himself to his feet and extended a hand to help her up. "Why don't we get you upstairs."

As stupid as she felt right now, she was having such a nice time talking to him that she hated to actually go to her room. But it was late, and he probably had more important things to do than to entertain her in the short amount of evening that remained. He'd already sacrificed most of his day for her.

She took his hand and he hiked her up, but as he pulled her to her feet her phone slipped from her hand and this time she actually did drop it. It landed in the grass between them. She and Marcus bent to pick it up at the exact same time, their heads colliding in the process. Hard.

They muttered a simultaneous "Ow."

She straightened and reached up to touch the impact point just above her left eye, wincing when her fingers brushed a tender spot. Great, now she could look forward to a hangover *and* a concussion. Could she make an even bigger ass of herself?

"You're hurt," he said, looking worried, which made her feel even stupider.

"I'm fine. It's just a little tender."

"Let me see," he insisted, gently cradling her cheek in his palm, turning her toward the light for a better look. With his other hand he brushed her hair aside, his fingertips grazing her forehead.

Her heart fell to the pit of her stomach, then lunged upward into her throat. *Oh my god.* If her legs had been a little wobbly before, her senses slightly compromised, that was *nothing* compared to the head-to-toe, limb-weakening, mind-altering, knock-me-off-my-feet rush of sensation she was experiencing now. His face was so close she could feel his breath whisper across her cheek, and the urge to reach up and run her hand across his stubbled chin was almost irresistible.

Her breath caught and she got a funny feeling in the pit of her stomach. Then his eyes dropped to hers and what she saw in them made her knees go weak.

He wanted her. *Really* wanted her.

Don't do it, Vanessa. Don't even think *about it.*

"Does it hurt?" he asked, but it came out as a raspy whisper.

The only thing hurting right now—other than her bruised pride—was her heart, for what she knew was about to happen. For the betrayal she would feel when she talked to Gabriel tomorrow. But even that wasn't enough to jar her back to reality. She invited the kiss, begged for it even, lifted her chin as he dipped his head, and when his lips brushed hers…

Perfection.

It was the kind of first kiss every girl dreamed of. Indescribable really. Every silly cliché and romantic platitude all rolled in one. And even though it had probably been inevitable, they simply could not let it happen again. To let it happen at all had been…well, there was no justification for it. To say it was a mistake was putting it mildly. But the problem was, it didn't *feel* like a mistake. She felt a bit as though this was the first smart thing, the first *right* thing, she had done in years.

Which is probably why she was *still* kissing him. Why her arms were around his neck, her fingers curled into his hair. And why she would have kept on kissing him if Marcus hadn't backed away and said, "I can't believe I just did that."

Which made her feel even worse.

She pressed a hand to her tingling lips. They were still damp, still tasted like him. Her heart was still pounding, her knees weak. He'd *wrecked* her.

Marcus looked sick with guilt. Very much, she imagined, how she probably looked. She had betrayed Gabriel. With his own *son*. What kind of depraved person was she?

A slap to the face couldn't have sobered her faster.

"It's not your fault. I let you," she said.

"Why did you?" he asked, and she could see in his eyes that he wanted some sort of answer as to why this was happening, why they were feeling this way.

"Because…" she began, then paused. She could diffuse the situation. She could tell him that she was just lonely, or he reminded her so much of Gabriel that she was confused. But it felt wrong to lie, and there was only one honest answer to give him. "Because I wanted you to."

He took a second to process that, looking as though he couldn't decide if it was a good or a bad thing, if he should feel relieved that it wasn't all his fault, or even more guilty. "If it was something I did—"

"It wasn't!" she assured him. "I mean, it was, but it was me too. It was both of us. We're obviously just, confused, or…*something*. And it would probably be best if we don't analyze it to death. I mean, what would be the point? It doesn't matter why we did it. We know that we shouldn't have, and even more important, we know that it can't happen again. Right?"

"Right."

"So that's that?"

He was quiet for several long seconds and she waited for his confirmation, because they really needed to put an end to this now.

But instead of agreeing with her, Marcus shook his head and said, "Maybe not."

Though it seemed impossible that a heart could both sink and lift at the same time, hers managed it. "Why not?"

"Because maybe if we figure out why we did it, I'll stop feeling like I want to do it again."

Marcus watched Vanessa struggle for what to say next, feeling a bit as though he were caught up in some racy evening television drama. This sort of thing didn't happen in real life. Not in civilized society anyway. Men did not have affairs with their fathers' female companions, and that was exactly what he thinking of doing.

What was *wrong* with him?

She'd admitted that she was not *in* love with his father, nor was she physically attracted to him. And Marcus truly believed they would never marry. But until Vanessa's relationship with his father was completely over, he had no right to lay a finger on her. Even then a relationship with her could potentially come between him and his father.

Not that he even *wanted* a relationship. After Carmela, he had vowed to practice the single life for a while. Like his father he was probably just rebounding, and this strange fascination was probably fleeting. He would be wise to remember that.

Like father, like son, right?

"Marcus—"

"No, you're right," he interrupted. "This was a mistake. I promise it won't happen again."

"Okay," she said, but he couldn't tell if she was relieved, or disappointed. Or if she even believed him. He wasn't sure if he believed himself.

They walked in silence up to her room, and she must have sobered up, because she was steadier now. When they reached her door she turned to him.

"I had a really good time tonight. I enjoyed our talk."

"So did I."

"And…well, thank you."

He wasn't quite sure what she was thanking him for, but he nodded anyway.

Without a backward glance, she stepped into her room and closed the door, and for a full minute Marcus just stood there, plagued with the sensation that nothing had been resolved, feeling the overpowering urge to knock on her door. The only problem was, he had no idea what he wanted to say to her.

That should have been the end of it, but something wasn't right. He just couldn't put his finger on what.

You're losing your mind, he thought with a bitter laugh, then he turned and walked down the hall. He pulled out the cell phone from his pocket, with the private number that not even Cleo knew about, and tapped on the outgoing calls icon. Vanessa's number popped up. Though he wasn't sure why he did it, he programmed the number into his address book, then stuck the phone back in his pocket.

Tomorrow would be better, he assured himself. Considering how stressful the past few months had been, and the fact that he'd been sleeping—on a good night—four or five restless hours, it was no wonder he wasn't thinking clearly. His physician had offered a prescription for sleeping pills, but Marcus was against taking medication unless absolutely necessary. The meditation that Cleo had suggested hadn't helped much either. There were times, especially in the evening, when he felt a bit as if he were walking around in a fog.

Tonight I'll sleep, he told himself, then things would be clearer in the morning. Instead, he laid in bed, tossing and turning, unable to keep his mind off Vanessa and the kiss that never should have happened. He drifted in and out of sleep, his dreams filled with hazy images that made no sense, but left him feeling edgy and restless.

Marcus dragged himself out of bed at 6 a.m. with thoughts and feelings just as jumbled as the day before. He showered, dressed and had breakfast, then he tried to concentrate on work for a while, but his mind kept wandering back to Vanessa and Mia. George had informed him that they went down to use the pool around eleven, and though he found himself wanting to join them, he knew it was a bad idea. Thinking that it might help to get away for the afternoon, he called a few acquaintances to see if anyone was free for lunch, but everyone was either busy or didn't answer their phone. Instead he ate his lunch from a tray in his suite while he read the newspaper, but after he was finished he went right back to feeling restless.

"Laps," he said to himself. Swimming laps always relieved stress. He didn't even know for sure that Vanessa was still down there. It was past one-thirty, so wouldn't Mia be due for a nap? Besides, maybe it was best to confront these feelings head-on, prove to himself that he was strong enough to resist this.

He dressed in his swimsuit, pulled on a shirt and headed down to the pool. He stepped out into the blistering afternoon heat to find that Vanessa was still there, in the water, her hair pulled back in a ponytail, not a stitch of makeup on her face. In that instant the emptiness melted away, replaced by a longing, a desire to be close to her that made it difficult to breathe. And all he could think was, *Marcus, you are in big trouble*.

Vanessa carried Mia around the shallow end of the pool, swishing her back and forth while Mia plunged her little fists into the water, giggling and squealing, delighting in the fact that she was splashing them both in the face. After what had turned out to be a long and restless night, all Vanessa really wanted to do was collapse in a lounge chair and doze the afternoon away. Thinking, of course, about anything but last night's kiss. Which she could do if she called Karin, but Mia was having so much fun, Vanessa hated to take her out of the water.

Deep down she knew it was a good thing that Marcus had decided not to join them today. Still, she couldn't deny the jerk of disappointment every time she looked over at

the door and he didn't come through it. Maybe, like her,
he just needed a day or two to cool down. Or maybe it had
nothing to do with that, and he just had more important
things to do. Either way, by lunchtime she had resigned
herself to the fact that he wasn't going to show. Of course
that still hadn't stopped her from looking over at the door
every five minutes, just in case.

"I guess today we're on our own," she told Mia.

"You two look like you're having fun."

Vanessa nearly jumped out of her skin at the unexpected voice, and whipped around to see Marcus walking
toward the pool, wearing nothing but a shirt and a little
black Speedo.

Holy cow.

Her heart plunged to her knees, then shot back up into
her throat, and she snapped her mouth shut before her jaw
had a chance to drop open. Did the man not own a pair of
swim trunks? The baggy variety that hung to the knee?

"Hi there!" she said, hoping she came across as friendly,
without sounding too enthusiastic. Mia, on the other hand,
heard his voice and practically dislocated her neck trying
to turn and see him, and when she got a glimpse of him
she let out a screech and batted at the water excitedly.

Marcus sat on the edge of the pool, dipping his feet in
the water, putting his crotch exactly at eye level, and with
his knees slightly spread, it was difficult not to stare.

"It's a hot one," he said, shading his eyes to look up at
the clear blue sky.

It certainly was, and she wasn't referring to the weather.
Maybe wishing he were in the pool with them had been
a bad idea. Her gaze wandered to his mouth, which of
course made her think about that kiss last night, and what
they might have done if they kept kissing. If she invited
him into her room.

Disaster, that's what would have happened. As it stood, the damage they had done wasn't irreparable. She could write it off as a serious lapse in judgment. Another kiss, and that may have been no longer the case.

Mia on the other hand had no shame. She practically jumped out of Vanessa's arms trying to reach him.

Vanessa laughed. "I think she wants you to come in."

He pushed off the edge and slid into the water, looking even better wet. But on the bright side, she didn't have to look at as much of him.

Mia reached for him and Marcus asked, "May I?"

"Of course," she said, handing Mia over.

He held her tightly to his bare chest, as if he were afraid he might drop her, and all Vanessa could think was, *you lucky kid.* But Mia wiggled in Marcus's arms, trying to get closer to the water.

"If you turn her around and hook your arm across her belly she can play in the water," Vanessa told Marcus, and the second he turned her, she began to splash and squeal.

"It's okay if the water gets in her eyes?" he asked, looking concerned.

"Are you kidding, she loves it. She does the same thing in the bathtub. You wouldn't believe the mess she makes. When she's all soapy it's a lot like trying to bathe a squid."

"She's pretty slippery without the soap too," Marcus said, but he was grinning.

"If you want to put her in her floating ring she likes to be pulled around the pool. The faster the better." Vanessa grabbed the ring from the side and Mia shrieked.

Marcus laughed. "Let's give it a try."

Vanessa held the ring still while Marcus maneuvered her inside, which, with all of her squirming, was a bit like wrestling a baby octopus. When she was securely seated, he tugged her across the pool, swimming backward into the deeper water, then he spun her in circles and Mia giggled and swung her arms, beside herself with joy. It warmed her heart, but also broke it a little, to see Mia so attached to him.

She backed up against the edge of the pool and just watched them.

"She really does like this," Marcus said, looking as if he was having just as much fun.

"She loves being in the water. I wish I had more time to take her swimming, but our complex back home doesn't have a pool. I could take her to the hotel, but if I dare show my face on my day off, I inevitably get wrangled into working."

"Maybe she'll be a champion swimmer someday," Marcus said.

"Gabriel told me you used to compete."

"I was working toward a spot on the Olympic team, which meant intense training. I swam at least fifteen to twenty thousand meters a day, plus weight training and jogging."

"Wow, that is intense."

"Yeah, and it began to interfere with my royal duties, so I had to give it up. Now it's just a good way to stay in shape."

It certainly was, she thought, admiring all the lean muscle in his arms and shoulders. "It's sad that you weren't able to follow your dream."

"I was disappointed, but not devastated. My life was just meant for different things."

"It must have been really amazing growing up with all this," she said, looking up at the palace.

"Well, it didn't suck," Marcus said with a grin, all dimples and white teeth.

Vanessa laughed. Sometimes it was easy to forget that

he was a future king. He just seemed so…ordinary. Gabriel, though just as approachable, had a more serious and formal manner. His confidence, his sense of self-worth, had been intoxicating, and a little thrilling. Even if he had doubts about his abilities as king he would never admit them. And though Marcus possessed that same air of conviction, he wasn't afraid or ashamed to show vulnerability, and there was something unbelievably sexy about that. Especially for a woman like her, who was constantly second-guessing herself.

"The truth is, I was away at boarding school for the better part of my childhood," Marcus said. "But I did come home for school breaks and summer vacations."

"I'm not sure if I could do that," Vanessa said.

"Go to boarding school?"

"Send my child away to be raised by someone else. It would break my heart."

"In my family it's just what was expected, I guess. It was the same for my father, and his father before him."

"But not your mother, right? She didn't mind letting you go?"

"I know she missed me, but as I said, that's just the way things were. She had her duties as queen, and I had mine."

Vanessa had a sudden heart-wrenching thought. "If I marry your father, would I have to send Mia away to boarding school?"

For several seconds he looked as if he wasn't sure how to answer, or if she could handle the truth.

"I can only assume that's what he would want," he finally said.

"And if I refused?"

"She's your child, Vanessa. You should raise her the way you see fit."

But if Gabriel were to adopt her, then Mia would be

both of theirs. Which he had already said would be an eventuality. Until just this moment, she had only imagined that as a good thing. Now she wasn't so sure. What if they had contrasting views about raising children? And suppose they had a baby together? Would she have even less control then?

"I guess that's just another thing we'll have to discuss when he gets back," she said, then for reasons she didn't fully understand, heard herself ask, "How would you feel about sending your children away to school?"

Why would she ask such a thing when his opinions about child-rearing had no bearing on her life in the least?

"I guess I've never really considered that," Marcus said. "I suppose it would be something I would have to discuss with my wife."

She couldn't help but wonder if he was just giving her the PC answer, or if he really meant it. And honestly, why did it matter?

Eleven

Vanessa heard her phone ringing from the chair where she'd set her things. Thinking that it might be Gabriel, she pushed herself up out of the pool and rushed to grab it, the intense afternoon heat drying her skin in the few seconds it took to reach it. Her heart sank when she saw her father's number on the display. She had played over in her mind about a million times what she would say to him when he finally called, yet she was still too chicken to answer. She let the call go to voice mail, waited until her alert chimed, then listened to the message.

"Hey Nessy, it's Daddy," he said and she cringed, in part because she was a grown woman and he still referred to himself as Daddy, and also because she absolutely hated being called Nessy. It made her sound as though she belonged in a Scottish loch. "I thought I might catch you before you left for work. I just called to tell you that my platoon reunion will be in Los Angeles next week so I'm flying in."

Oh, crap. She closed her eyes and sighed.

"The reunion is a week from Friday night and I want time to see my grandbaby, so I'll be taking a flight early Thursday morning."

He wasn't coming there to see Vanessa, just Mia. Ironic considering he'd barely acknowledged her existence until she was almost three months old. Before then he referred to her as Vanessa's *latest mistake*. Knowing how disappointed he would be, she hadn't even told him she was pregnant until it was no longer possible to hide it. And when she had, he'd responded in that same tired, disappointed tone, "Vanessa, when will you learn?"

"I'll call with my flight information when I get it," his message said. "You can swing by and pick me up from the airport. See you soon!"

He never asked, he only demanded. Suppose she'd had other plans? Or was it that he just didn't care? It wasn't unlike him to visit on a whim and expect her to drop everything and entertain him. She had to endure that same old look of disappointment when she didn't cater to his every whim. It had always been that way, even when she was a kid. God forbid if she didn't get the laundry washed and ironed and the dishes done, not to mention the vacuuming and the dusting and the grocery shopping. And of course she was expected to maintain straight As in school. He ran a tight ship, and she had been expected to fall in line. And he wondered why she lit out of there the day she graduated high school. Which was, of course, another mistake.

This time she wouldn't be there to disappoint him… which in itself would be a disappointment, she supposed. The truth is, no matter what she did, in his opinion it would never be the right thing.

She sighed and dropped the phone back onto the chair, then looked up, surprised to find Marcus and Mia floating near the edge watching her.

"Everything okay?" he asked.

She forced a smile. "Sure. Fine."

"You're lying," he said.

She went for an innocent look, but was pretty sure it came out looking more like a grimace. "Why would you think that?"

"Because you're chewing on your thumbnail, and people generally do that when they're nervous."

She looked down to find she'd chewed off the tip of her left thumbnail. Damn. He didn't miss a thing, did he? And the way he was looking up at her, she began to wonder if choosing her bikini over the conservative one-piece had been a bad idea. She felt so…exposed, yet at the same time, she *liked* that he was looking at her. She *wanted* him to.

Vanessa, that is just so wrong.

"It's fine if you don't want to talk about it," he said.

She sat on the edge of the pool, dipping her feet in the water. "My father just left a message. He's coming to Los Angeles to visit next week."

"Does that mean you'll be leaving?"

The old Vanessa may have. She would have been worried about disappointing him yet again. But she was twenty-four years old, damn it. It was time to cut the umbilical cord and live her life the way she wanted. But she was the new Vanessa now, and that Vanessa was confident and strong and no longer cared what her father thought.

She hoped so at least.

"I'm not leaving," she told Marcus. "I'm going to call him back and tell him that I won't be there, and we'll have to reschedule for another time."

"And when he asks where you are?"

That was the tricky part.

"I'll tell him the truth." Maybe.

You're strong, she reminded herself. *You are responsible for your own destiny and what he thinks doesn't matter.*

And if she told herself enough times, she just might start to believe it.

Marcus stood behind Vanessa while she examined an exhibit at the museum, thinking that of all the visitors he had escorted there over the years—and there had been many—she showed by far the most intense interest. She didn't just politely browse while looking bored out of her skull. She absorbed information, reading every sign and description carefully, as if she were dedicating it to memory.

"You do realize that there's no quiz when we get back to the palace," he teased, as she read the fine print on a display of artifacts from the Varieo civil war of 1899.

She smiled sheepishly. "I'm taking forever, I know, but I just love history. It was my favorite subject in school."

"I don't mind," he told her, and he honestly didn't. Just like he hadn't minded spending the afternoon at the pool with her and Mia the day before. And not because of that hot pink bikini she'd worn. Okay, not completely because of the bikini. He just…liked her.

"I just wish Mia would sit in her stroller," Vanessa said, hiking her daughter, who had been unusually fidgety and fussy all day, higher on her hip. "She desperately needs a nap." But every time Vanessa tried to strap her into the stroller Mia would begin to howl.

"Why don't you let me hold her for a while," he said, extending his arms. Mia lunged for him.

"Jeez, kid!" Laughing, Vanessa handed her over, and

when Mia instantly settled against his shoulder, said, "She sure does like you."

The feeling was mutual. He even sort of liked having a baby around the palace. Although the idea that this little person could become his stepsister was a strange one. Not that he believed it would ever really happen. But did that possibly mean he was ready to start a family of his own? Eight months ago he would have said absolutely not. But so much had changed since then. He felt as if he'd changed, and he knew for a fact that it had everything to do with Vanessa's visit.

They walked to the next display, where Vanessa seemed intent on memorizing the name of every battle and its respective date. He stood behind her to the left, watching her, memorizing the curve of her face, the delicate shell of her ear, wishing he could reach out and touch her. He felt that way all the time lately, and the impulse was getting more difficult to ignore. And he knew, by the way she looked at him, the way her face flushed when they were close, the way her breath caught when he took her hand to help her out of the car, she felt it too.

When she was finished, she turned to Marcus, looked at him and laughed.

"What are you? The baby whisperer?"

He looked down at Mia to find that she was sleeping soundly on his shoulder. "Well, you said she needed a nap."

"You could try sitting her in the stroller now."

"I don't mind holding her."

"Are you sure?"

"Why risk waking her," he said, but the truth was, he just liked holding her. And he'd been doing it a lot more often. Yesterday he'd carried her on his shoulders as they strolled down the stretch of private beach at the marina— Vanessa wearing that ridiculous floppy hat—and Mia delighted in tugging on handfuls of his hair. Later they sat on a blanket close to the shore and let Mia play in the sand and splash in the salty water. Those simple activities had made him feel happier, feel more *human*, than he had in ages.

With Mia asleep in his arms, they turned and walked toward the next section of the museum.

"You're really good with her," Vanessa said. "Are you around kids much?"

"I have a few friends with young children, but I don't see them very often."

"The friends, or the children?"

"Either, really. Since we lost my mother I haven't felt much like socializing. The only time I see people now is at formal events where I'm bound by duty to attend, and children, especially small ones, are not typically included on the guest list."

She gazed up at him, looking sad. "It sounds lonely."

"What does?"

"Your life. Everyone needs friends. Would your mother be happy if she knew how you've isolated yourself?"

"No, she wouldn't. But the only true friend I had betrayed me. Sometimes I think I'm better off alone."

"I could be your friend," she said. "And having experienced firsthand what it feels like to be betrayed by a friend, you can trust that I would never do that to you."

Despite everything he'd learned of her the past three days, the blunt statement still surprised him. And he couldn't help but wonder if that might be a bad idea, that if being her friend would only strengthen the physical attraction he felt growing nearly every time he looked at her, every time she opened her mouth and all that honesty spilled out. Which is why he shouldn't have said what he said next.

"In that case, would you care to join me for dinner on the veranda tonight?"

The invitation seemed to surprise her. "Um, yeah, I'd love to. What time?"

"How about eight?"

"Mia goes to bed right around then, so that would be perfect. And I assume you mean the veranda in the west wing, off the dining room?"

"That's the one. I see you've been studying your map."

"Since I'm going to be here a while either way, I should probably learn my way around." She glanced at her watch, frowned and said, "Wow, I didn't realize how late it is. Maybe we should think about getting back."

"I'm in no hurry if you want to stay."

"I really do need to get back," she said, looking uncomfortable. "Gabriel promised to Skype me at four today, so…"

So she obviously was looking forward to speaking to him. And was that jealousy he was feeling? He forced a smile and kept his tone nonchalant. "Well then, by all means, let's go."

You have no reason to be nervous, Vanessa told herself for the tenth time since she'd left her room and made her way to the veranda. They'd spent all day together and though it had been a little awkward at times, Marcus had been a perfect gentleman, and she was sure tonight would be no exception. He probably only invited her to dinner because he felt obligated to entertain her. Or maybe he really did want to be friends.

And what a sophomoric thing that had been to say to him, she thought, offering to be his friend. As if he probably didn't already have tons of people lining up to be his friend. What made her so special?

Or was that just her way of subtly telling him that's all they could ever be. Friends. And she was sure that with time, she would stop fantasizing about him taking her in his arms, kissing her, then tearing off her clothes and making passionate love to her. Tearing, because he wasn't the kind of man to take things slow. He would be hot and sexy and demanding and she would of course have multiple orgasms. At least, in her fantasy she did. The fantasy she had been playing over and over in her head since he'd kissed her.

Get a grip, Vanessa. You're only making this harder on yourself.

She found the dining room and stepped through the open doors onto the veranda at exactly seven fifty-nine. Taper candles burned in fresh floral centerpieces on a round bistro table set for two, and champagne chilled in an ice bucket beside it. Beyond the veranda, past lush, sweetly scented flower gardens, the setting sun was a stunning palette of brilliant red and orange streaking an indigo canvas sky. A mild breeze swept away the afternoon heat.

It was the ideal setting for a romantic dinner. But this was supposed to be a meal shared between friends. Wasn't it?

"I see you found it."

She spun around to find Marcus standing behind her. He stood leaning casually in the dining room doorway, hands tucked into the front pockets of his slacks, his white silk shirt a stark contrast to his deep olive skin and his jacket the exact same rich espresso shade as his eyes. His hair was combed back but one stubborn wavy lock caressed his forehead.

"Wow, you look really nice," she said, instantly wishing she could take the words back. *This is a casual dinner* between *friends,* she reminded herself. She shouldn't be chucking out personal compliments.

"You sound surprised," he said with a raised brow.

"No! Of course not. I just meant…" She realized Marcus was grinning. He was teasing her. She gestured to the sleeveless, coral-colored slip dress she was wearing. She had wanted to look nice, without appearing blatantly sexy, and this was the only dress she'd brought with her that seemed to fit the bill. It was simple, and shapeless without looking frumpy. "I wasn't really sure how formal to dress."

His eyes raked over her. Blatantly, and with no shame. "You look lovely."

He said it politely, but the hunger in his gaze, and the resulting tug of lust deep in her belly, was anything but polite. And as exposed as she felt just then, she might as well have been wearing a transparent negligee, or nothing at all. And the worst part was, she liked it. She liked the way she felt when he looked at her. Even though it was so very wrong.

He gestured to the table. "Shall we sit?"

She nodded, and he helped her into her chair, the backs of his fingers brushing her bare shoulders as he eased it to the table, and she actually shivered. Honest to goodness goose bumps broke out across her skin.

Oh my.

She'd read in stories about a man making a woman shiver just by touching her, but it had never actually happened to her. In fact, she thought the whole thing sounded sort of silly. Not so much anymore.

"Champagne?" Marcus asked.

Oh, that could be a really bad idea. The last thing she needed was something to compromise her senses. They were compromised enough already. But the bottle was open, and she hated to let good champagne—and noting the label, it was *good* champagne—go to waste.

"Just one glass," she heard herself say, knowing she would have to be careful not to let one glass become two and so on.

Marcus poured it himself, then took a seat across from her. He lifted his glass, pinned his eyes on her and said, "To my father."

There was some sort of message in his eyes, but for the life of her, she wasn't sure what it was. Was toasting his father his way of letting her know the boundaries they'd established were still firmly in place, or did it mean something else entirely?

She'd just as soon they didn't talk about Gabriel at all. And rather than analyze it to death, she lifted her own glass and said, "To Gabriel." Hoping that would be the end of it.

She took a tiny sip, then set her glass down, and before she could even begin to think of what to say next, one of the younger butlers appeared with a gleaming silver tray and served the soup. He even nodded cordially when she thanked him. Karin definitely seemed to be warming to her as well, and Vanessa's maid had actually smiled and said good morning when she came in to make the bed that morning. They weren't exactly rolling out the red carpet—more like flopping down the welcome mat—but it was progress.

The soup consisted of bite-sized dumplings swimming in some sort of rich beef broth. And it was delicious. But that didn't surprise her considering the food had been exemplary since she arrived.

"You spoke with my father today?" he asked.

Ugh, she really didn't want to do this, but she nodded. "This afternoon."

"He told you that my aunt is still in intensive care?"

"He said she had a bad night. That her fever spiked, and she may need surgery. It sounds as if he won't be home anytime soon." Despite what she had hoped.

"He told me she's still very ill," Marcus said, then his eyes lifted to hers. "He asked if I've been keeping you entertained."

Oh, he had definitely been doing that.

"He asked if I've been respectful."

Her heart skipped a beat. "You don't think he…"

"Suspects something?" Marcus said bluntly, then he shook his head. "No. I think he's still worried that I won't be nice to you."

Oh, he'd been "nice" all right. A little too nice, some might say.

"He said you seemed reluctant to talk about me."

The truth was, she hadn't known what to tell Gabriel. She worried that if she said too much, like mentioning the earrings, or their evening stroll, Gabriel might get suspicious. She didn't know what was considered proper, and what was pushing the boundaries, so she figured it was better not to say anything at all. "I didn't mean to be elusive, or give him the impression I felt unwelcome."

"I just don't want him to think that I've neglected my duty," Marcus said.

"Of course. I'll be sure to let him know that you've been a good host."

They both quietly ate their soup for several minutes, then Marcus asked, "Have you spoken with your father yet?"

She lowered her eyes to her bowl. "Uh, nope, not yet."

She took a taste of her soup and when she looked up, he was pinning her with one of those brow-tipped stares.

"I *will*," she said.

"The longer you wait, the harder it will be."

She set her spoon down, her belly suddenly knotted with nerves. She lifted her glass and took another sip. "I know. I just have to work up the nerve. I'll do it, I just…I need to wait until the time is right."

"Which will happen when?"

When he was at the airport waiting for her to pick him up, maybe. "I'll do it. Probably tomorrow. The problem is, whenever I have the time, it's the middle of the night there."

The brow rose higher.

She sighed. "Okay, that's a lie. I'm a big fat chicken. There, I said it."

One of the butlers appeared to clear their soup plates. While another served the salad, Vanessa's phone started to ring. Would it be funny—not ha-ha funny, but ironic funny—if that were him right now.

She pulled it out of her pocketbook and saw that it wasn't her father, but Karin. As crabby as Mia had been today, maybe she was having trouble getting her to settle.

"Mia woke with a fever, ma'am."

It wasn't unusual for Mia to run a low-grade fever when she was teething, and that would explain her foul mood. "Did you take her temperature?"

"Yes, ma'am. It's forty point five."

The number confused her for a second, then she realized Karin meant Celsius. She racked her brain to recall the conversion and came up with a frighteningly high number. Over one hundred and *four* degrees!

She felt the color drain from her face. Could that be right? And if it was, this was no case of teething. "I'll be right up."

Marcus must have seen the fear in her eyes, because he frowned and asked, "What's wrong?"

Vanessa was already out of her chair. "It's Mia. She has a fever. A high one."

Marcus shoved himself to his feet, pulled out his phone and dialed. "George, please get Dr. Stark on the line and tell him we need him immediately."

Twelve

Other than a mild cold in the spring, Mia had never really been sick a day in her life. Imagining the worst, Vanessa's heart pounded a mile a minute as she rushed up the stairs to her suite, Marcus trailing close behind. When she reached the nursery she flung the door open.

Karin had stripped Mia down to her diaper and was rocking her gently, patting her back. Mia's cheeks were bright red and her eyelids droopy, and Vanessa's heart sank even lower as she crossed the room to her. How, in a couple of hours' time, could she have gotten so sick?

"Hey, baby," Vanessa said, touching Mia's forehead. It was burning hot. "Did you give her anything?"

Karin shook her head. "No, ma'am. I called you the minute she woke up."

Vanessa took Mia from her. She was limp and listless. "In the bathroom there's a bottle of acetaminophen drops. Could you get it for me, please?"

Karin scurried off and Marcus, who stood by the door looking worried, asked, "Is there anything I can do?"

"Just get the doctor up here as fast as possible." She cradled Mia to her chest, her hands trembling she was so frightened.

Karin hurried back with the drops and Vanessa measured out the correct dose. Mia swallowed it without a fuss.

"I don't know what this could be. She's barely ever had a cold."

"I'm sure it's nothing serious. Probably just a virus."

"I wonder if I should put her in a cool bath to bring her temperature down."

"How high is it?"

"Over one hundred and four."

His brows flew up.

"Fahrenheit," she added, and his face relaxed.

"Why don't you wait and see what the doctor says?"

She checked the clock across the room. "How soon do you think he'll be here?"

"Quickly. He's on call 24/7."

"Is he a pediatrician?"

"A family practitioner, but I assure you he is more than qualified."

She didn't imagine the royal family would keep an unqualified physician on call.

"Why don't you sit down," Marcus said, gesturing to the rocker. "Children can sense when parents are upset."

He was right, she needed to pull it together. The way the baby lay limp in Vanessa's arms, whimpering pathetically, it was as if she didn't have the energy to cry. She sat in the chair, cradling Mia in her arms and rocked her gently. "I'm sorry to have interrupted dinner. You can go back down and finish."

He folded his arms. "I'm not going anywhere."

Though she was used to handling things on her own when it came to her daughter, she was grateful for his company. Sometimes she got tired of being alone.

Dr. Stark, a kind-faced older gentleman, arrived just a few minutes later carrying a black medical bag.

He shook her hand and asked in English, "How old is the child?"

"Six months."

"Healthy?"

"Usually, yes. The worst she's ever had was a mild cold. I don't know why she would have such a high fever."

"She's current on her vaccinations?"

She nodded.

"You flew here recently?"

"Five days ago."

He nodded, touching Mia's forehead. "You have records?"

She was confused for a second, then realized he meant medical records. "Yes, in my bedroom."

"I'd like to see them."

Marcus held out his arms. "I'll hold her while you get them."

She handed her to him and Mia went without a fuss.

She darted across the hall to her room, grabbed the file with Mia's medical and immunization records, then hurried back to the bedroom. Marcus was sitting in the rocking chair, cradling Mia against his shoulder. Karin stood by the door looking concerned.

"Here they are," she said, and the doctor took the folder from her.

He skimmed the file then set it aside. "You'll need to lay her down."

Marcus rose from the chair and set Mia down on the changing table with all the care and affection of a father, watching with concern as the doctor gave her a thorough exam, asking random questions. When he looked in her ears she started to fuss.

When he was finished, Vanessa asked, "Is it serious?"

"She'll be fine," he assured her, patting her arm. "As I suspected, it's just an ear infection."

Vanessa was so relieved she could have cried. She picked Mia up and held her tight. "How could she have gotten that?"

"It could have started as a virus. A round of antibiotics should clear it right up. The acetaminophen you gave her should bring the fever down."

It looked as if it already had started to work. Mia's cheeks weren't as red and her eyes seemed less droopy. "Could that be why she was so crabby during the flight here?"

"I doubt it. Some children are just sensitive to the cabin pressure. It could have been hurting her ears."

It broke her heart to think that all the time they'd been in the air, Mia had been in pain and Vanessa hadn't even known it. "What can I do to keep it from happening in the future?"

"I would keep her out of the air until the infection clears, then, when you fly home, try earplugs. It will help regulate the pressure."

If she went home, that is. She glanced over at Marcus, who was looking at her. Was he thinking the same thing?

"Right now the best thing for her is a good night's rest. I'll have the antibiotics delivered right away. Just follow the directions. Call if she hasn't improved by morning. Otherwise I'll check her again in two days."

"Thank you, Dr. Stark," she said, shaking his hand.

"Shall I put her back in her crib?" Karin asked Vanessa after he left.

Vanessa shook her head. "I'm going to take her to my room, so you can have the night off. Thanks for calling me so quickly."

Karin nodded and started to walk to her room, then she stopped, turned back and said, "She's a strong girl, she'll be fine in no time." Then she actually smiled.

When she was gone, Vanessa turned to Marcus. He'd removed his jacket and was leaning against the wall, arms crossed. "Thank you," she said.

He cocked his head slightly. "For what?"

"Getting the doctor here so fast. For just being here with me. I don't suppose you have a portable crib anywhere around here. She rolls so much that I get nervous keeping her in bed with me."

Marcus pulled out his phone. "I'm sure we have one."

The medicine arrived fifteen minutes later and Vanessa gave her a dose, and within half an hour a portable crib had been set up in her bedroom. Vanessa laid Mia, who had fallen asleep on her shoulder, inside and covered her with a light blanket. She gently touched Mia's forehead, relieved to find that her temperature had returned almost to normal.

She walked back out into the sitting room where Marcus waited. It was dark but for a lamp on the desk. He stood by the French doors, the curtain pulled back, gazing into the night. Her first instinct was to walk up to him, slide her arms around his waist and lay her head against his back. She imagined that they would stay that way for a while, then he would turn and take her in his arms, kiss her the way he did the other night.

But as much as she wanted to—ached for it even—she couldn't do it.

"She's in bed," she said, and Marcus turned to her, letting the curtain drop. "I think she's better already."

"That's good."

The phone on her desk began to ring and she crossed the room to pick it up. It was Gabriel. Thank goodness he couldn't see her face or surely he would recognize the guilt there for the thoughts she had just been having.

"George called," he said, sounding worried. "He told me that Mia is ill."

"She woke with a fever."

"The doctor was there?"

"He came right away. It's an ear infection. He put her on antibiotics."

"What can I do? Do you need me to come home? I can catch a flight first thing in the morning."

This was it. She could say yes, and get Gabriel back here and be done with this whole crazy thing with Marcus. Instead she heard herself saying, "In the time it would take you to get here, she'll probably be fine. Her fever is already down."

"Are you sure?"

"Trina needs you more than I do. Besides, Marcus is helping," she said, glancing his way.

His expression was unreadable.

"Call me if you need anything, day or night," Gabriel said.

"I will, I promise."

"I'll let you go so you can tend to her needs. I'll call you tomorrow."

"Okay."

"Good night, sweet Vanessa. I love you."

"I love you, too," she said, and she did. She loved him as a friend, so why did she feel like a fraud? And why did she feel so uncomfortable saying the words in front of Marcus?

Well, duh, of course she knew why.

She set the phone down and turned to Marcus. He stood

by the sofa, his arms folded across his chest. "Your father," she said, as if he needed an explanation.

"He offered to come home?" he asked.

She nodded.

"You told him no?"

She nodded again.

He started walking toward her. "Why? Isn't that what you wanted?"

"It was…I mean, it *is*. I just think…" The truth was, she was afraid. Afraid that Gabriel would come home, see her face and instantly know what she was feeling for Marcus. He trusted her, *loved* her, and she'd betrayed him. And she continued to betray him every time she had an inappropriate thought about his son, but she just couldn't seem to stop herself. Or maybe she didn't want to stop. "Maybe we need some time to sort this out before he comes back."

"Sort what out?"

"This. Us."

"I thought there was no us. That we were going to pretend like it never happened."

That had seemed like a good idea yesterday, but now she wasn't so sure she could do that. Not right away, anyhow. "We are. I just…need some time to think."

He stepped closer, his dark eyes serious and pinned to hers. Her stomach bottomed out and her heart started to beat faster.

"Please don't look at me like that."

"Like what?"

"Like you want to kiss me again."

"But I do."

Oh boy. Her knees felt squishy. "You know that would be a really bad idea."

"Yeah, it probably would."

"You really shouldn't."

"So tell me no."

He wanted *her* to be the responsible one? Seriously?

"Have you not heard a thing I've said this week?"

"Every word of it."

"Then you know that you really shouldn't trust me with a responsibility like that, considering my tendency to make bad decisions."

His grin warmed her from the inside out. "Right now, I'm sort of counting on it."

Thirteen

Vanessa reached up and cupped Marcus's cheek, running her thumb across that adorable dimple, something she'd wanted to do since the first time she'd seen him smile.

This was completely insane, what they were about to do, because she knew in her heart that this time it wouldn't just be a kiss. But with him standing right in front of her, gazing into her eyes with that hungry look, she just couldn't make herself stop him. And her last thought, as he lowered his head and leaned in, as she rose up to meet him halfway, was how wrong this was, and how absolutely wonderful.

Then he kissed her. But this time it was different, this kiss had a mutual urgency that said neither would be having a crisis of conscience. In a weird way it felt as if they had been working toward this moment since the minute she'd stepped off the plane. Like somewhere deep down she just knew it had been inevitable. It was difficult to imagine that at one time she hadn't even liked him. A big fat jerk, that's what she'd thought him to be. She'd been so wrong about him. About so many things.

"I want you Vanessa," he whispered against her lips. "I don't care if it's wrong."

She pulled back to look him in the eyes. How could she have known this beautiful man only five days when right now it felt like an eternity?

And right now their feelings were the only ones that mattered to her.

She shoved his jacket off his shoulders, down his arms, and it dropped to the floor. She ran her hands up the front of his shirt, over his muscular chest, the way she had wanted to since he stood in her doorway that day with his shirt unbuttoned. And he felt just as good as she knew he would.

Marcus groaned deep in his throat. Then, as if the last bit of his control snapped, he kissed her hard, lifting her off her feet and pinning her to the wall with the length of his body. She gasped against his lips, hooked her legs around his hips, curling her fingers into the meat of his arms. This was the Marcus she had fantasized about, the one who would sweep her off her feet and take her with reckless abandon, and everything inside her screamed, "Yes!"

Marcus set her on her feet and grabbed the hem of her dress, yanking it up over her head—as close to tearing as he could get without actually shredding the delicate silk fabric. When she stood there in nothing but a bra and panties, he stopped and just looked at her.

"You're amazing," he said.

Not beautiful, but amazing. Was it possible that he really did see more in her than just a pretty face? When she looked at Marcus she saw not royalty, not a prince, but a man who was charismatic and kind and funny. And maybe a little vulnerable too. A man who was looking back at her with the same deep affection. Could it be that her feelings for Gabriel were never meant to be more than friendship? That Marcus was the one she was destined to fall in love with? Because as much as she'd tried to fight it, she was definitely falling in love with him.

She took his hand and walked backward to the sofa, tugging him along with her. A part of her said that she should have been second-guessing herself, or feeling guilty—and a week ago, she probably would have—but as they undressed, kissing and touching each other, it just felt right.

When he was naked, she took a moment to just look at him. Physically he was just as perfect as he could possibly be, but she didn't really care about that. It was his mind that fascinated her most, who he was on the inside.

She lay back against the sofa, pulling him down with her, so he was cradled between her thighs. He grinned down at her, brushing her hair back from her face. "You know that this is completely crazy."

"I know. I take it you don't do crazy things?"

"Never."

"Me neither." She stroked the sides of his face, his neck, ran her hands across his shoulders. She just couldn't stop touching him. "Maybe that's why this feels so good. Maybe we both need a little crazy."

"That must be it." He leaned down to kiss her, but just as his lips brushed hers, he stopped, uttering a curse.

"If you're about to tell me we have to stop, I'm going to be very upset," she said.

"No, I just realized, I don't have protection with me."

"You *don't?* Aren't princes supposed to be prepared at all times?" She paused, frowning. "Or is that the scouts?"

"I wasn't exactly planning for this, you know."

"Really?"

He laughed. "Yes, really. But then you walked into the room wearing that dress…"

"*That* dress? Are you kidding me? It's like the least sexy thing I own. I wore it so I *wouldn't* tempt you."

"The truth is, you could have been wearing a paper sack and I would have wanted to rip it off you. It's you that I want, not your clothes."

It was thrilling to know he wanted her that much, that he would be attracted to her even at her worst.

"I'm going to have to run back to my room," he said, not sounding at all thrilled with the idea.

"I'm on birth control, so you don't have to."

"Are you sure?"

"I'm sure. And now that we have that settled, could we stop talking and get to the good stuff?"

He grinned. "I thought women liked to talk."

"Yes, but even we have our limits."

She didn't have to ask twice, and lying there with him, kissing and touching, felt completely natural. There was none of the usual first time fumbling or awkwardness. And any vestige of reservations, or hint of mixed feelings that may have remained evaporated the instant he thrust inside her. Everything else in the world, any cares or worries or feelings of indecision that were always there somewhere in the back of her mind, melted away. She knew from the instant he began to move inside her—slow and gentle at first, then harder and faster, until it got so out of control they tumbled off the couch onto the rug—that this was meant to be. He made her feel the way a woman was supposed to feel. Adored and desired and protected, and *strong*, as if no one or no thing could ever knock her back down.

And she felt heartbroken, all the way down to her soul,

because as much as she wanted Marcus, she couldn't have him, and she was terrified that no man would ever make her feel this way again.

"We're totally screwed, aren't we?" Vanessa asked Marcus, lying next to him naked on the floor beside the sofa, her breath just as raspy and uneven as his own, glowing from what had been for him some of the best sex of his entire life. Actually no, it had been *the* best.

Maybe it was the anticipation that had made it so exciting, or the forbidden nature of the relationship. Maybe it was that she had no hang-ups about her looks or insecurities about her body, or that she gave herself heart and soul and held nothing back. It could have been that unlike most women, whatever she took, she gave back tenfold.

Or maybe he just really liked her.

At this point, what difference did it make? Because she was right. They were screwed. How could he possibly explain this to his father? "Sorry, but I just slept with the woman you love, and I think I might be falling in love with her myself, but don't worry, you'll find someone else."

There was a code among men when it came to girlfriends and wives, and that was even more true among family. It was a line a man simply did not cross. But he had crossed it, and the worst part was that he couldn't seem to make himself feel guilty about it.

"My father can't ever know," he said.

She nodded. "I know. And I can't marry him now."

"I know." He felt bad about that, but maybe it was for the best. He believed that Vanessa came here with the very best of intentions, but she obviously didn't love his father the way a wife loves a husband. Maybe by stepping between them Marcus had done them both a favor. Vanessa was so sweet and kind, he could imagine her compromising her own happiness to make his father happy. Eventually though, they would have both been miserable. In essence, he had saved them from an inevitable failed marriage.

Or was he just trying to rationalize a situation that was completely irrational?

She reached down and laced her fingers through his. "It's not your fault that this happened, so please don't ever blame yourself."

He squeezed her hand. "It's no one's fault. Sometimes things just…happen. It doesn't have to make sense."

She looked over at him. "You know that no matter how we feel, you and I, we can't ever…"

"I know." And the thought caused an actual pain in his chest. A longing so deep he felt hollowed out and raw. He had little doubt that Vanessa was the one for him. She was his destiny, she *and* Mia, but he could never have them. Not if he ever hoped to have a civilized relationship with his father. It was as if the universe was playing a cruel trick on them. But in his world honor reigned supreme, and family always came first. His feelings, his happiness, were inconsequential.

It wasn't fair, but when was life ever?

"I need to call him and tell him," Vanessa said. "That it's over, I mean. I won't tell him about us."

The minute she ended her relationship with his father, she would have to leave. There would be no justifiable reason to stay. And the idea that this was it, that Marcus would never be with Vanessa again, that he had to give her up so soon, made his heart pound and adrenaline rush. He wasn't ready to let her go. Not yet.

"That's not the sort of thing that you should do over the phone, or through Skype," he told her. "Shouldn't you wait until he returns?"

Her brow furrowed into a frown. "It just doesn't seem

fair to let him think that everything is okay, then dump him the second he gets back. That just seems…cruel."

And this was the woman he'd been convinced was a devious gold digger. How could he have been so wrong? Because he was an idiot, or at least, he had been. And he would be again if he let her go now.

"Do you really think now is the right time?" he said, grasping for a reason, any reason, to get her to stay. "He's so upset over my aunt."

She blinked. "I guess I hadn't really thought about it that way. That would be pretty thoughtless. But I don't think I can wait until he comes back. That could be weeks still."

"Then at least wait until she's out of intensive care."

"I don't know…"

Oh, to hell with this. Here she was being honest and he was trying to manipulate her.

"The truth is, I don't care about my father's feelings. This is pure selfishness. Because the minute you tell him, it's over, and I just can't let you go yet." He pulled her close, cupped her face in his hands. "Stay with me, Vanessa. Just a few days more."

She looked conflicted, and sad. "You know we'll just be torturing ourselves."

"I don't care. I just want a little more time with you." Not wanted. *Needed.* And he had never needed anyone in his life.

"We would have to be discreet. No one can know. If Gabriel found out—"

"He won't. I promise."

She hesitated a moment, then smiled and touched his cheek. "Okay. A few more days."

He breathed a quiet sigh of relief. Was this wrong in more ways than he could count, and were they just delaying the inevitable? Of course. And did he care? Not really.

He'd spent his entire life making sacrifices, catering to the whims of others. This one time he was going to be selfish, take something for himself.

"But then I have to go," she said. "I have to get on with my life."

"I understand." Because he did too, as difficult as that was to imagine. But for now she was his, and he planned to make the most of what little time they had left together.

"You did what?" Jessy shrieked into the phone, so loud that Vanessa had to hold it away from her ear. "I don't talk to you for a couple of days and this happens?"

Vanessa cringed. Maybe telling Jessy that she'd slept with Marcus, several times now, hadn't been such a hot idea after all. But if she didn't tell *someone,* she felt as if she would burst.

"You realize I was kidding when I suggested he could be a viable second choice," Jessy said.

"I know. And it's not something I planned on happening."

"He didn't, you know...*force* you."

"God no! Of course not. What is your hang-up about the men in this country being brutes?"

"I'm just worried about you."

"Well, don't be. Marcus would never do that. He's one of the sweetest and kindest men I've ever met. It was one hundred percent mutual."

"But you've barely known him a week. You don't sleep with guys you've known a week. Hell, sometimes you make them wait *months*."

"I know. And it's a wonder we held out as long as we did."

Jessy laughed. "Oh my God. Who are you and what have you done with my best friend?"

"I know, this isn't like me at all. And the weird thing is, if I could go back and do it differently, I wouldn't. I'm glad for what happened. And I'm glad I met him. It's changed me."

"In five days?"

"It sounds impossible, I know. I have a hard time believing it myself, but I just feel *different*. I feel…gosh, I don't know, like a better person, I guess."

Jessy laughed again. "You're sleeping with the son of the man you're supposed to marry, and you feel like a better person?"

It did sound weird when she said it like that. "It's hard to explain. And though I hate to admit it, I think what you said about Gabriel being a father figure was true. Nothing I do is good enough for my dad, and I guess in a way I transferred my feelings onto Gabriel. Deep down I knew that I didn't love him the way a wife should love a husband, that I never would. But he seemed to love me so much, and I didn't want to let him down. But then I met Marcus and something just…clicked. If it hadn't been for him, I may have made another terrible mistake."

"So you must really like him."

If only it were that simple. "That would be a major understatement."

Jessy was quiet for a second, then she said, "Are you saying that you *love* him? After *five* days?"

"Weird, huh?"

"How does he feel?"

She shrugged. "What does it matter?"

"It seems to me like it would matter an awful lot."

If only. "We can't be together. How do you think Gabriel would feel if I told him I was dumping him for his son? He might never forgive Marcus."

"You don't think Marcus would choose you over his father?"

"It doesn't matter because I would never ask him to. Nor would I want him to. Family and honor mean everything to Marcus. It's one of the things I love most about him."

"So, the thing you love most is what's keeping you apart."

"I guess so, yeah." And the thought of leaving, of giving him up, filled her belly with painful knots, and she knew that the longer she stayed the worse it would be when she left, yet here she still was. "This is making me sad. Let's talk about something else. How was your trip?"

"It was good," Jessy said, sounding surprised. "It was actually…fun."

"His family is nice?"

"Yeah. They're very small-town, if you know what I mean, and very traditional. Wayne and I had to sleep in separate rooms. They have this big old farmhouse with lots of land and though I've always been more of a city girl, it was really beautiful. Hot as hell though."

Vanessa smiled. "I'm really glad that it went well."

At least one of them was in a relationship that might actually work.

"I know you don't want to talk about it," Jessy said, "but can I just say one more thing about your affair with the prince?"

Vanessa sighed. "Okay."

"This is going to sound strange. But I'm proud of you."

It was Vanessa who laughed this time. "I slept with the son of the man I was planning to marry and you're *proud* of me?"

"You're always so hell-bent on making other people happy, but you did something selfish, something for yourself. That's a huge step for you."

"I guess I never thought of being selfish as a good thing."

"Sometimes it is."

"You know what the hardest part about leaving will be? Mia has become so attached to him, and he really seems to love her. I think he would be an awesome dad."

"You'll meet someone else, Vanessa. You'll fall in love again, I promise."

Vanessa wasn't so sure about that. In her entire life she'd never felt this way about anyone, she hadn't even known it was possible to love someone the way she loved Marcus. To need someone as much as she needed him, yet feel more free than she had in her life. And she just couldn't imagine it ever happening again. What if Marcus was it? What if he was her destiny? Was it also her destiny to let him go?

Fourteen

Vanessa woke to another message from her father, the third one that he had left in as many days, this one sounding more gruff and irritated than the last two.

"Nessy, why haven't you called me back? I called the hotel and they said you took a leave of absence. I want to know what's going on. Have you gotten yourself into trouble again?"

Of course that would be his first assumption, that she had done something wrong. What else would he think? She sighed, not so disappointed as she was resigned to the way things were. And a little sad that he always seemed to see the worst in her.

"Call me as soon as you get this," he demanded, and that's where the message ended. She dropped her phone on the bedside table and fell back against the pillows.

Beside her, Marcus stirred, waking slowly, the way he always did. Or at least, the last three mornings when they woke up together, he had. First he stretched, lengthening every inch of that long, lean body, then he yawned deeply, and finally he opened his eyes, saw her lying there next to him, and gave her a sleepy smile, his hair all rumpled and sexy. Creases from his pillow lined his cheek.

Watching this ritual had become her new favorite way to spend her morning. Even though what they were doing still filled her with guilt. She just couldn't seem to stay away.

"What time is it?" he asked in a voice still gravelly from sleep.

"Almost eight."

He rolled onto his back and laughed, the covers sliding down to expose his beautiful bare chest. "That makes last night the third night in a row that I slept over seven hours straight. Do you have any idea how long it's been since I got a decent night's sleep?"

"I'm that boring, huh?"

He grinned and pulled her on top of him, so she was straddling his thighs, his beard stubble rough against her chin as he kissed her. "More like you're wearing me out."

It had rained the past two days and Marcus had decided it would be best to spend them in the palace, in her suite. Wearing as little clothing as possible. They mostly just talked, and played with Mia, and when Mia took her naps, they spent the entire time making love. A few times Vanessa had even let Karin watch Mia for an extra hour or so, so they had a little more time together. And though it had been a week now, neither Vanessa nor Marcus had brought up the subject of her leaving, but it loomed between them, unspoken. A dark shadow and a constant element of shame that hung over what had been—other than Mia's birth—the best time of her life. She kept telling herself that when the time was right to leave, they would just know it. So far that time hadn't come, and deep down she wished it never would.

Marcus was it for her. He was the one, her *soul mate,* and of that she was one hundred and ten percent sure. For the first time in her life she had no doubts. She wasn't second-guessing herself, or worrying that she was making a mistake.

She wasn't exactly sure if he felt the same way. He seemed to, and he clearly didn't want her to leave, but did he love her? He hadn't actually said so. But to be fair, neither had she. At this point, what difference did it make? They were just words. Even if he did love her, his relationship with his father *had* to come first.

After that first time making love, she'd dreaded having to face Gabriel on Skype, sure that he would know the second he saw her face, but while she waited on her computer for over an hour, he'd been a no-show. She'd been more relieved than anything. He'd phoned the next day, apologizing, complaining of security issues, and said it might be better if they limited their calls to voice only. Which actually worked out pretty well for her. Already she could feel herself pulling away.

Their conversations were shorter now, and more superficial. And one day, when Marcus had taken them for a drive to see the royal family's mountain cabin—although to call the lavish vacation home a cabin was akin to calling the Louvre a cute little art gallery—she'd been out of cell range and had missed his call completely. She hadn't even remembered to check for a message. And though it was clearly her fault that they hadn't spoken, he had been the one to apologize the next day. He said he was swamped with work and tending to Trina, and he hadn't had a chance to call back.

She kept waiting for him to ask her if there was a problem, but if he had noticed any change in their relationship, he hadn't mentioned it yet. But Trina had been improving, and though she was still very weak, and Gabriel hadn't felt comfortable leaving her yet, it was only a matter of time.

And then of course she had her father to deal with.

"You look troubled," Marcus said, brushing her hair back and tucking it behind her ear.

He had an uncanny way of always knowing what she was thinking. "My dad called again."

He sighed. "That would explain it."

"He called the hotel and found out that I took a leave, so of course he's assuming that I'm in some sort of trouble. He demanded that I call him immediately."

"You should. You should have called him days ago."

"I know." She let out a sigh and draped herself across his warm, solid chest, pressing her ear to the center, to hear the thump of his heart beating.

"So do it now."

"I don't want to."

"Stop acting like a coward and just call him."

She sat up and looked down at him. "I'm acting like a coward because I *am* one."

"No, you aren't."

Yes, she was. When it came to dealing with her father anyway. "I'll call him tomorrow. I promise."

"You'll call him now," he said, dumping her off his lap and onto the mattress. Then he got up and walked to the bathroom, all naked and gorgeous, his tight behind looking so squeezable.

He stopped in the doorway, turned to her and grinned. "Now, I'm going to take a shower, and if you want to join me, you had better start dialing."

The door closed behind him, then she heard the shower switch on. Damn him. He knew how much she loved taking their morning shower together. He brought a change of clothes to her room every night so no one would see him the next morning wearing the same clothes from the night before. He also rolled around in his bed and mussed up the covers so it would look as if he'd slept there. It had to be obvious to pretty much everyone how much time they had been spending together, but if anyone suspected inappropriate behavior, they'd kept it to themselves.

Vanessa sighed and looked over at the bathroom door, then her phone. Well, here goes nothing.

She sat up, grabbed it and dialed her father's number before she chickened out. He answered on the first ring. "Nessy, where the hell have you been? I've been worried sick. Where's Mia? Is she okay?"

He'd been worried sick about both of them, or just Mia, she wondered. "Sorry, Dad, I would have called you sooner but I've actually been out of the country."

"Out of the country?" he barked, as if that were some unforgivable crime. "Why didn't you tell me? And where is my granddaughter?"

"She's with me."

"Where are you?" he said, sounding no less irate. She knew he was only acting this way because he was worried, and he hated not being in control of every situation every minute. If she gave him hourly reports of her activities he would be ecstatic. And usually when he spoke to her this way it made her feel about two inches tall. Right now, she just felt annoyed.

"I'm in Varieo, you know that little country near—"

"I *know* where it is. What in God's name are you doing there?"

"It's sort of…a work thing." Because she had met Gabriel at work, right?

"I thought you took a leave from the hotel. Or was that just a fancy way of saying they fired you?"

Of course he would think that.

Her annoyance multiplied by fifty. "No, I was not *fired*," she snapped.

"Do not take that tone with me, young lady," he barked back at her.

Young lady? Was she *five*?

In that instant something inside of her snapped and she'd had enough of being treated like an irresponsible child. And if standing up for herself meant disappointing him, so be it. "I'm twenty-four, Dad. I'll take whatever tone I damned well please. And for the record, I deserve the same respect that you demand from me. I am sick to death of you talking down to me, and always thinking the worst of me. And I'm finished with you making me feel as if anything I do is never good enough for you. I'm smart, and successful, and brave, and I have lots of friends and people who love me. So unless you can think of something positive to say to me, don't bother calling anymore."

She disconnected the call, and even though her heart was thumping, and her hands were trembling, she felt... good. In fact, she felt pretty freaking fantastic. Maybe Marcus was right. Maybe she really was brave. And though she didn't honestly believe this would change anything, at least now he knew how she felt.

Her phone began to ring and she jerked with surprise. It was her dad. She was tempted to let it go to voice mail, but she'd started this, and she needed to finish it.

Bracing herself for the inevitable shouting, she answered. "Hello."

"I'm sorry."

Her jaw actually dropped. "W-what?"

"I said I'm sorry," he repeated, and she'd never heard

him sound so humbled. She couldn't recall a single time he'd ever apologized for anything.

"And I'm sorry I raised my voice," she said, then realized that she had done nothing wrong. "Actually, no, I'm not sorry. You deserved it."

"You're right. I had no right to snap at you like that. But when I didn't hear from you, I was just afraid that something bad had happened to you."

"I'm fine. Mia is fine. And I'm sorry that I frightened you. We're here visiting a…friend."

"I didn't know you had any friends there."

"I met him at the hotel. He was a guest."

"He?"

"Yes, he. He's…" Oh what the hell, why not just tell him the truth? Since she didn't really care what he thought at this point anyway. "He's the king."

"The *king?*"

"Yes, and believe it or not, he wants to marry me."

"You're getting married? To a king?" He actually sounded excited. He was finally happy about something she had done, and now she had to burst his bubble. Figures.

"He wants me to marry him, but I'm not going to."

"Why not?"

"Because I'm in love with someone else."

"Another king," he joked.

"Um, no."

"Then who?"

If he was going to blow his top, this would be the time. "I'm in love with the prince. His son."

"Vanessa!"

She braced herself for the fireworks. For the shouting and the berating, but it never happened. She could practically feel the tension through the phone line, but he didn't make a sound. He must have been biting a hole right through his tongue. And could she blame him? Sometimes even she couldn't believe what they were doing.

"You okay, Dad?"

"Just...confused. When did all this happen? *How* did it happen?"

"Like I said, he was visiting the hotel and we became friends."

"The king or the prince?"

"The king, Gabriel, and he fell in love with me, but I only ever loved him as a friend. But he was convinced I would grow to love him if I got to know him better, so he invited me to stay at the palace, but then he was called away when I got here. He asked Marcus—he's the prince—to be my companion and we...well, we fell for each other. Hard."

"How old is this prince?"

"Um, twenty-eight, I think."

"And the king?"

"Fifty-six," she said, and she could practically hear him chomping down on his tongue again. "Which was part of the reason I wasn't sure about marrying him."

"I see," was all he said, but she knew he wanted to say more. He was going to need stitches by the end of this conversation. But she gave him credit for making the effort, and she wished she had confronted him years ago. Though he probably hadn't been ready to hear it before now. Or maybe she was the one who hadn't been ready for this. Maybe she needed to make changes first.

"So, I assume you'll be marrying the prince instead?" he said.

If only. "I won't be marrying anybody."

"But I thought you love him."

"I do love him, but I could never do that to Gabriel. He's a really good man, Dad, and he's been through so much heartache. He loves me, and I could never betray him that way. I feel horrible that it worked out this way, as if I've let him down. Not to mention that it would most likely ruin his relationship with his son. I couldn't do that to either of them. They need each other more than they need me."

He was quiet for several seconds, then he said, "Well, you've had a busy couple of weeks, haven't you?"

Though normally a comment like that would come off as bitter or condescending, now he just sounded surprised. She smiled, feeling both happy and sad, which seemed to be a regular thing for her lately. "You have no idea."

"So I guess I won't be seeing you Thursday."

"No, but we should be flying home soon. Maybe we can make a quick stop in Florida on our way."

"I'd like that." He paused and said, "So you really love this guy?"

"I really love him. Mia does too. She's grown so attached to him, and she loves being here in the palace."

"Are you sure you're doing the right thing? By leaving, I mean."

"There isn't anything else that I can do."

"Well, I'll keep my fingers crossed that you work it out somehow. And Nessy, I know I've been pretty hard on you, and maybe I don't say it often enough, but I am proud of you."

She'd waited an awfully long time to hear that, and as good as it felt, her entire self-worth no longer depended on it. "Thanks, Dad."

"It's admirable what you're doing. Sacrificing your own happiness for the king's feelings."

"I'm not doing it to be admirable."

"I know. That's why it is. Give me a call when you're coming home and I'll get the guest room ready."

"I will. I love you, Dad."

"I love you too, Nessy."

She hung up and set her phone on the table, thinking that was probably one of the nicest things her dad had ever said to her, and one of the most civilized conversations they had ever had.

"Now aren't you glad you called?"

She looked up to find Marcus standing naked in the bathroom doorway, towel-drying his hair. She wondered how much of that he'd heard. Had he heard her tell her father that she loved Marcus?

"I confronted him about the way he makes me feel, and instead of freaking out, he actually apologized."

"That took guts."

"Maybe I am brave after all. I'm not naive enough to think it will be smooth sailing from here. I'm sure he'll have relapses, because that's just who he is, and I'll have to stand firm. But at least it's a start."

He dropped the towel and walked toward the bed. And my goodness he looked hot. The man just oozed sex appeal. It boggled the mind that a woman would be unfaithful to him. His ex must have been out of her mind.

He yanked the covers away and climbed into bed, tugging her down onto her back, spreading her thighs with his knee and making himself comfortable between them.

"Thank you," she said, running her hand across his smooth, just shaved cheek. "Thank you for making me believe in myself."

"That wasn't me," he said, kissing her gently. His lips were soft and tasted like mint. "I just pointed out what was already there. You chose to see it."

And without him she might never have. She was a different person now. A better person. In part because of him.

"There's one more thing," he said, kissing her chin, her throat, the shell of her ear.

She closed her eyes and sighed. "Hmm?"

"For the record," he whispered, "I love you, too."

Fifteen

After a week of torrential rain the weather finally broke and though Marcus would have been more than happy to spend the day in Vanessa's suite again, sunny skies and mild temperatures lured them back out into the world. A calm sea made it the perfect day for water sports, and since Vanessa had never been on a personal watercraft, he figured it was time she learned.

They left Mia with Karin, who he thought looked relieved to have something to do. Many of the young parents he knew took full advantage of their nannies—especially the fathers, to the point that they'd never even changed a diaper—but Vanessa was very much a hands-on parent. He had the feeling Karin was bored more often than not. And because Mia was usually with them, they always took the limo on their outings, so today he decided they would take *his* baby for a spin.

"This looks really old," Vanessa said, as he opened the

passenger door, which for her was on the wrong side of the car.

"It's a 1965. It was my grandfather's. He was a huge Ian Fleming fan."

"Oh my God! Is this—"

"An Aston Martin DB5 Saloon," he said. "An exact replica of the car 007 drove."

She slipped inside, running her hand along the dash, as gently as a lover's caress. "It's amazing!"

He walked around and climbed in. He started the engine, which still purred as sweetly as the day they drove it off the line, put it in gear and steered the car through the open gates, and in the direction of the marina. "I've always loved this car. My grandfather and I used to sneak off on Sundays and drive out into the country for hours. He would tell me stories about his childhood. He was only nineteen when his father died, and he would tell me what it was like to be a king at such a young age. At the time, I just thought it sounded exciting to be so important and have everyone look up to you. Only as I got older and began to learn how much hard work was involved did I begin to realize what a huge responsibility it would be. I used to worry that my father would die and I would be king before I was ready."

"How old was your father when he became king?"

"Forty-three."

She was quiet for a minute, then she turned to him and said, "Let's not go to the marina. Let's take a drive in the country instead. Like you and your grandfather used to do."

"Really?"

"Yeah. I would love to see the places he took you."

"You wouldn't be bored?"

She reached over, took his hand, and smiled, "With you, never."

"Okay, let's go."

He couldn't recall ever getting in a car with a woman and just driving. In his experience they preferred constant stimulation and entertainment, and required lavish gifts and attention. In contrast, Vanessa seemed to relish the times they simply sat around and talked, or played with her daughter. And as far as gifts go, besides the earrings—which she wore every day—he'd bought nothing but the occasional meal or snack. She required little, demanded nothing, yet gave more of herself than he could ever ask. Before now, he hadn't even known women like her existed. That he once thought she had ulterior motives was ridiculous to him now.

"Can I ask you a question?" she said, and he nodded. "When did you stop thinking that I was after your dad's money?"

And she was apparently a mind reader. "It was when we went to the village and you didn't once use the credit card my father left for you."

Her mouth dropped open in surprise. "You knew about that?"

"His assistant told me. She was concerned."

"Gabriel insisted that I use it, but the truth is I haven't even taken it out of the drawer. It didn't seem right. He gave me lots of gifts, and I insisted he take them back."

"Well, if the credit card hadn't convinced me, your reaction to the earrings really drove the message home."

She reached up to finger the silver swirls dangling from her ears. "Why?"

"Because I've never seen a woman so thrilled over such an inexpensive gift."

"Value has nothing to do with it. It's the thought that counts. You bought them because you wanted to, because you knew that I liked them. You weren't trying to buy my

affections or win me over. You bought the earrings because you're a sweet guy."

He glared at her. "I am not sweet."

She grinned. "Yes, you are. You're one of the sweetest,
kindest men I've ever met." She paused, gave his hand a
squeeze. "You know I have to go soon. I've probably stayed
too long already. I feel like we're tempting fate, like someone is going to figure out what we're doing and it will get
back to Gabriel. I don't want to hurt him."

Though it was irrational, he almost wished it would.
He didn't want to hurt his father either, but it was get-
ting more and more difficult to imagine letting her go.
He wasn't even sure if he could. "What if he did find out?
Maybe you wouldn't have to leave. Maybe we could ex-
plain to him. Make him understand."

She closed her eyes and sighed. "I can't, Marcus. I can't
do that to him. Or to you. If our relationship came between
the two of you I would never forgive myself."

"We don't know for certain that he would be upset."

She shot him a look.

"Okay, he probably would, but he could get over it. In
fact, when he sees how much it means to me, I'm sure he
will."

"But what if he doesn't? That isn't a chance I'm willing to take."

If she were anything like the women he'd dated in the
past, this wouldn't be an issue. She wouldn't care who she
hurt as long as she got what she wanted. Of course, then
he wouldn't love her. And he knew that once she'd made
up her mind, nothing would change it.

Her stubborn streak was one of her most frustrating yet
endearing qualities. He liked that she continually chal-
lenged him. She kept him honest. And he loved her too
much to risk losing her respect.

* * *

After a three-hour drive that they spent talking about their childhoods and families, then a stop in a small village for lunch, Marcus drove them back to the palace. He walked with her up to the nursery, only to discover that Mia had just gone down for a nap.

"Just call me when she wakes up," Vanessa told Karin, then she turned to Marcus and gave him the *look,* the one that said she had naughtiness on her mind. He followed her across the hall, but stopped her just outside her suite door.

"How about a change of pace?"

"What did you have in mind?" she asked, looking intrigued.

"Let's go to my room."

The smile slipped from her face. "Marcus…"

"But you've never even seen it."

"If someone sees us go in there—"

"The family wing is very private. And if you want, we won't do anything but talk. We can even leave the door open. We can pretend like I'm giving you a tour of the family wing."

She looked hesitant. "I don't know."

Despite the risk of being discovered by a passing employee, he took her hand. "We haven't got much time left. Give me the chance to share at least a small part of my life with you."

He could see her melting before his eyes. Finally she smiled and said, "Okay."

What he hadn't told was that just the other day Cleo had confronted him about all the time they had been spending together.

"Talk to my father," he'd told Cleo. "He's the one who wanted me to keep her entertained."

Her brows rose. "Entertained?"

"You *know* what I mean."

She flashed him a told-you-so smile. "I take it you're finding that she's not as terrible as you thought?"

"Not terrible at all," he'd told her, diffusing the situation entirely. Because if she believed the relationship was platonic, no one on the staff, except maybe George, would question it. But he still didn't dare tell Vanessa about the exchange. Especially now.

Under the ruse of tour guide, Marcus led Vanessa through the palace to the family wing, and the employees they did encounter only bowed politely, and showed not even a hint of suspicion. When they got to his suite, the hall was deserted. He opened the door and gestured her inside.

"Wow," she said, walking to the center of the living room and gazing around. He stood by the open door watching her take it all in. "It's huge. As big as an apartment. You even have a kitchen."

"I insisted. I figured, if I have to live here in the palace, I need a space of my own."

"I like it. It's very tasteful, and masculine without being too overpowering." She turned to him. "Comfortable."

"Thank you. And my designer thanks you."

"How many rooms?"

"Master suite, office, kitchen and living room."

She nodded slowly. "It's nice."

"I'm glad you like it."

She dropped her purse on the leather sofa and turned to him. "Maybe you should close the door."

"But I thought we agreed—"

"Close the door, Marcus." She was wearing that look again, so he closed it. "Lock it too."

He locked it, and crossed the room to where she was standing. "Changed your mind, did you?"

She slid her hands up his chest, started unfastening the

buttons on his shirt. "Maybe it's the element of danger, but the closer we got to your room, the more turned on I got." She rose up on her toes and kissed him, yanking his shirt from the waist of his slacks. "Or maybe, when we're alone, I just can't keep my hands off you."

The feeling was mutual.

"I know it's wrong, but I just can't stop myself. Doesn't that make me a terrible person?"

"If it does, I'm a terrible person, too. Which could very well mean we deserve each other."

She tugged his shirt off, but before she could get to work on his belt, he picked her up and hoisted her over his shoulder. She let out a screech of surprise, then laughed.

"Marcus, what are you doing!"

"Manhandling you," he said, carrying her to the bedroom and kicking the door open.

"Not that I mind, but why?"

He tossed her down onto the bed, on top of the duvet, then he reached under her dress, hooked his fingers in the waist of her panties and yanked them down. "Because I am not *sweet*."

She grinned up at him. "Well, I stand corrected."

Then she grabbed him by the shoulders, pulled him down on top of her and kissed him.

Every time he made love to her he thought it couldn't possibly get better, but she always managed to top herself. She was sexy and adventurous, and completely confident in her abilities as a lover, and *modest* was a word not even in her vocabulary. She seemed to instinctively know exactly what to do to drive him out of his mind, and she was so damned easy to please—she had a sensitive spot behind her knees that if stroked just right would set her off like a rocket.

She liked it slow and sensual, hard and fast, and she

even went a little kinky on him at times. If there were an ideal sexual mate for everyone, there was no doubt in his mind that she was his. And each time they made love that became more clear.

Maybe, he thought, as she unfastened his pants, it was less about skill, and more about the intense feelings of love and affection they shared. But then she slid her hand inside his boxers, wrapped it around his erection and slowly stroked him, and his thoughts became all hazy and muddled. She made it so easy to forget the world around him, to focus on her and her alone. And he wondered what it would be like this time, slow and tender or maybe hot and sweaty. Or would she get that mischievous twinkle in her eyes and do something that would make most women blush?

Vanessa pushed him over onto his back and climbed on top of him, then she yanked her dress up over her head and tossed it onto the floor. Hot and sweaty, he thought with a grin—his particular favorite—and as she thrust against him, impaling herself on his erection, she was so hot and tight and wet, he stopped thinking altogether. And as they reached their climax together, then collapsed in each other's arms, he told himself that there had to be some way to talk her into staying.

And at the same time, his conscience asked the question: To what end?

Sixteen

Somewhere in the back of Marcus's mind he heard pounding.

What the hell was that? he wondered, and what could he do to make it stop? Then he realized, it was his door. Someone was knocking on his bedroom door.

His eyes flew open, and he tried to sit up, but there was a warm body draped across his chest. He and Vanessa must have fallen asleep. He looked over at the clock, and realized that it was past suppertime. Oh hell. No doubt Mia was awake by now.

He shook Vanessa. "Wake up!"

Her eyes fluttered open and she gave him a sleepy smile. "Hey."

"We fell asleep. It's late."

She shot up in bed and squinted at the clock, then she uttered a very unladylike curse. "Where's my phone? Mia must be awake by now. Why didn't Karin call me?"

The pounding started again as they both jumped out of bed.

"Who is that?" Vanessa asked, frantically looking around, he assumed, for her purse.

He tugged his pants on. "Stay here. I'll go see."

He rushed out to the living room, unlocked the door and yanked it open. Cleo's hand was in the air, poised to knock again.

"There you are!" she said.

"I was…taking a nap," he said, raking a hand through his tousled hair. "I haven't been sleeping well."

"Well, we have a problem. Poor Karin is frantic. Mia woke from her nap an hour ago but she can't find Vanessa. She's not answering her phone and I can't find her anywhere in the palace. I thought perhaps you knew where I might find her."

Was that suspicion in her eyes? "She probably went for a walk," Marcus said. "Maybe she forgot her phone."

"If she left the palace, security would know about it."

He opened his mouth to reply and she added, "But just in case, I had them check the gardens and she isn't out there. It's as if she disappeared."

"Give me a minute to get dressed and I'll find her."

Behind him Marcus heard an "oof!" then a loud crash. He swung around to find Vanessa on the floor by the couch, wrapped in a bed sheet, wincing and cradling her left foot. Beside her lay the floor lamp that had been standing there. Then he heard a noise from the hall and whipped back around to find that in his haste he'd pushed the door open, and Cleo could see the entire sordid scenario.

"Miss Reynolds," Cleo said, her jaw rigid. "Would you please call Karin and let her know that you are in fact fine, and haven't been abducted by terrorists?"

"Yes, ma'am," Vanessa said, her voice trembling, her cheeks crimson with shame.

Cleo turned to Marcus and said tightly, "A word in private, your highness?"

"Are you okay?" he asked Vanessa, who looked utterly miserable, and she nodded. "I'll be right back."

He stepped out into the hall, pulling the door closed behind him, and the look Cleo gave him curdled his blood.

"You lied to me?"

"What was I supposed to do? Tell you the truth? I can see how well that's going over."

"Marcus, what were you thinking?"

Had it been anyone but her berating him this way, he would have dismissed them on the spot. But Cleo had earned this right through years of loyal service. She was more an extension of family than an employee.

"Cleo, believe me when I say, we didn't plan for this to happen. And if it's any consolation, she's not going to marry my father."

"I should hope not! Your father deserves better than a woman who would—"

"This was not her fault," he said sharply, because he absolutely drew the line at any disparaging remarks against Vanessa. She didn't deserve it. "I pursued her."

"Look, Marcus," she said, touching his arm. "I know you're upset over Carmela, and maybe this is your way of getting revenge, but would you risk your relationship with your father for a—a cheap *fling?*"

"No, but I would for the woman who I've fallen hopelessly in love with."

She pulled her hand back in surprise. "You love her?"

"She's everything I have ever imagined I could want in a woman, and a few things I didn't even know I wanted until I met her. And she loves me too, which, considering my track record with women, is pretty damned astonishing. And the irony of it all is that those things I admire most about her are the reason we can never be together."

"You can't?"

"She thinks our relationship will come between me and my father, and she absolutely refuses to let that happen."

"You know that she's right."

"Sometimes I think that I don't even care. But she does, and as much as I'd like to, I would never go against her wishes."

Cleo shook her head. "I don't know what to say. I'm just…I'm so sorry things have to be this way."

"I can count on you to keep this conversation private," he said.

"Of course, Marcus."

He leaned down and kissed her papery cheek. "Thanks."

He stepped back into his suite, leaving her in the hall looking unbelievably sad.

Vanessa was dressed and sitting on the couch, putting her sandals on, when Marcus stepped back into the room. And from his expression she couldn't tell what had happened. "Marcus, I am so sorry."

"It's okay."

"I left my phone in my purse on the couch, that's why I didn't hear Karin calling me. Then I tripped on that stupid lamp. And I didn't mean to fall asleep."

"I fell asleep too. I take it Mia is okay."

"Fine. I figured we would need to talk, so I asked Karin to feed Mia her dinner and get her into bed for me."

He sat down on the couch beside her. "There's nothing to talk about. It's no one's fault."

No, they had plenty to talk about. "Cleo looked so… disappointed."

He sighed. "Yeah, she's good at that. But I explained the entire situation and she understands."

"That's not good enough."

"Vanessa—"

"I can't do this anymore, Marcus."

"I'm not ready for you to go."

"We knew this was inevitable. We kept saying that eventually the day would come that I'd have to leave. And I honestly think that it's here."

He squeezed her hand, gave her a sad smile. "I can't lose you. Not yet."

She shook her head. "My mind is made up. But I want you to know that this has been the happiest couple of weeks in my life, and I will never, as long as I live, forget you."

"Say you'll leave tomorrow. That you'll give me one more night."

She touched his cheek. It was rough from afternoon stubble. "I'm sorry. I just can't."

He leaned in to kiss her, and someone knocked on his door again. Marcus muttered a curse.

"Marcus, it's Cleo!"

"Come in!" he called, sounding exasperated, and he didn't even let go of her hand.

She opened the door and poked her head in. "I'm sorry to bother you again, but I thought you might like to know that your father's limo just pulled up out front. He's home."

Vanessa and Marcus uttered the same curse, at the exact same time, and bolted up off the couch.

"We'll be right down," he told Cleo, and snatched his shirt off the floor. He tugged it on and fastened the buttons, tucking it into his slacks. She was pretty sure he wasn't wearing any underwear, not that it made a difference at this point. Her hands were shaking so hard she was just glad she was already dressed.

He raked his fingers through his hair and asked, "You ready for this?"

She had always thought she was; now she wasn't so sure. She swallowed hard, shook her head.

"Me neither." He pulled her against him and kissed her. Long and slow and deep. Their last kiss. And he definitely made it a good one. Then he pulled away and said, "We'd better go."

They rushed down the stairs, Vanessa's legs feeling like limp noodles. That would be a sure way out of this disastrous situation. Trip on the stairs, tumble down and break her neck when she hit the marble floor below. Talk about taking the easy way out. But she managed to stay on her feet.

The instant her sandal hit the marble floor the front door swung open and Gabriel walked through. He was dressed casually in khaki pants and a polo shirt. Though she had expected him to look tired and pale from splitting his time between working and sitting at Trina's bedside, instead he looked tan and well rested, as if he'd been on an extended vacation.

He saw the two of them there and smiled. "Marcus, Vanessa."

He walked over and gave his son a hug, then shook his hand firmly. Then he turned to Vanessa.

"My sweet Vanessa," he said, taking her hands and grasping them firmly. "It's so good to see you."

She would have expected a much more enthusiastic greeting from a man who supposedly loved her. Or could it have just been that he didn't feel comfortable showing her physical affection in front of his son? That made sense. Whatever the reason she was actually grateful. If he had pulled her into his arms and kissed her passionately, that would have been awkward. And seeing Gabriel and Marcus there together, side by side, she realized that while they were definitely built similarly, and had the same dark tones, in looks Marcus actually favored his mother.

"I talked to you yesterday but you didn't say you were coming home," she told Gabriel.

"I thought I would surprise you."

Oh, she was definitely surprised.

"You have a bit of sunburn," Gabriel said, touching her chin lightly. "You've been getting outdoors."

Actually, she hadn't been out in the sun for days, how could she—? Beard burn, she realized, from the last time Marcus kissed her. So she lied and said, "Yes, we were outside just today."

"Where is Mia?" he asked.

"Upstairs, having her dinner."

"Good, good," he said, and something about his demeanor was just slightly…off. As if he were nervous. And she had never seen him nervous. Strangely enough, now that he was here in front of her, any trace of nerves she'd had were gone. She just felt sad. And though she would always love and respect him as a friend, any desire she may have had to marry him was gone. In this case absence did not make the heart grow fonder. She was too busy falling in love with someone else. And she couldn't put this off any longer. She had to end it now.

"Gabriel," she said, forcing a smile. "Can we talk? Privately, I mean."

"Yes, yes, of course. Why don't we go up to your suite." He turned to Marcus, whose jaw was so tight it could have snapped like a twig. "Please excuse us, son. We'll catch up later. I have news."

Marcus nodded. He was jealous, Vanessa could see it in his eyes, but he stayed silent. What choice did he have?

As they walked up the stairs together, Gabriel didn't even hold her hand, and he made idle chitchat, much the way he had during their recent phone conversations. When they got to her suite, she held her breath, scared to death that he might suddenly take her in his arms and kiss her, because the idea of pushing him away, of having to be so cruel, broke her heart. But he made no attempt to touch her, and when he gestured toward the sofa and asked her to sit down, he didn't even sit beside her. He sat across from her in the wing back chair. And he was definitely nervous. Had someone told him that they suspected her and Marcus of something inappropriate? And if he asked her for the truth, what should she say? Could she lie to him?

Or what if…*oh God*, was he going to *propose?*

"Gabriel, before you say anything, there's something I really need to tell you."

He rubbed his palms together. "And there's something I need to tell you."

"I'll go first," she said.

"No, it would be better if I did."

Vanessa leaned forward slightly. "Actually, it would probably be better if I did."

"No, mine is pretty important," he said, looking slightly annoyed.

"Well, so is mine," she said, feeling a little annoyed herself.

"Vanessa—"

"Gabriel—"

Then they said in perfect unison, "I can't marry you."

Seventeen

Marcus watched Vanessa and his father walk up the stairs together thinking, *what is wrong with this picture.*

If his father was happy to see her, why hadn't he kissed her? Why wasn't he holding her hand? And why had he looked so…nervous? He never got nervous.

"Something is up," Cleo said behind him, and he turned to her.

"So it's not just me who noticed."

"As giddy in love as he was when he came back from America, I thought he would sweep her into his arms the instant he walked in the door, then promptly drop to one knee to propose."

"Are you thinking what I'm thinking?" Marcus asked.

"He doesn't want to marry her."

Marcus was already moving toward the stairs when Cleo grabbed his sleeve.

"This doesn't mean he won't be angry, Marcus, or feel betrayed."

No, it didn't, but every time Marcus imagined Vanessa leaving he got a pain in his chest so sharp, it was as if someone had reached into his chest, grabbed his heart and was squeezing the life from him. The thought of watching her and Mia get on a plane, of seeing it take them away from Varieo forever, filled him with a feeling of panic so intense it was difficult to draw a breath.

He shrugged. "I don't care, Cleo. I can't do it. I can't let her go."

Cleo let go of his sleeve, and smiled up at him. "So what are you waiting for?"

He charged up the stairs to the second floor and raced down the hall to her room. Not even bothering to knock, he flung the door open. Vanessa was seated on the sofa, his father in the chair across from her, and the sudden intrusion surprised them both.

"Marcus," Vanessa said. "What are you doing here?"

"I need to have a word with my father," he told her.

His father frowned. "Is something wrong, son?"

"Yes and no. I guess it just depends on how you look at it."

Vanessa rose to her feet, shaking her head. "Marcus, don't—"

"I *have* to, Vanessa."

"But—"

"I know." He shrugged helplessly. "But I have to."

She sat back down, as if she'd gotten tired of fighting it too, and whatever happened, she was willing to live with the consequences.

"Marcus, can this wait? I really need to talk to Vanessa."

"No, it can't. What I need to tell you must be said right now."

His father looked to Vanessa, who sat there silently. "All right," he said, sounding annoyed. "Talk."

Marcus took a deep breath and blew it out, hoping his father would at least try to understand. "Remember when you thanked me for agreeing to spend time with Vanessa, and said in return, if I ever needed anything, to just ask?"

He nodded. "I remember."

"Did you really mean it?"

"Of course I did. I'm a man of my word. You know that."

"Then I need you to do something for me."

"Anything, Marcus."

"Let Vanessa go."

He drew back slightly, blinking in confusion. "Let her go? But…I just did. I just now told her that I couldn't marry her."

"That's not good enough. I need you to *really* let her go, forget you ever wanted to marry her."

He frowned. "Marcus, what on earth are you talking about? Why would I do that?"

"So I can marry her."

His father's mouth actually dropped open.

"You told me that Vanessa is a remarkable woman, and said that once I got to know her, I would love her. Well, you were right. I do love her." He turned to Vanessa. "More than she could possibly imagine. Too much to ever let her leave."

She smiled, tears filling her eyes. "I love you, too, Marcus."

He turned back to his father, who sat there looking stunned. "You have to understand that we didn't mean for this to happen, and we did fight it. But we just…" He shrugged. "We just couldn't help it."

"You had an affair," his father said, as if to clarify.

"This was no affair," Marcus said. "We fell in love."

"So," his father said, turning to Vanessa, "this is why you couldn't marry me?"

"Yes. I'm so sorry. But like Marcus said, we didn't mean for this to happen. At first, he didn't even like me."

His father slowly nodded, as though he were letting it sink in, but oddly enough, he didn't look angry. Maybe the depth of their betrayal had left him temporarily numb.

"We had agreed not to say anything, to end it," Marcus told him. "She was going to do the honorable thing and leave. Neither of us could bear the thought of hurting you. But I need her. Her and Mia."

His father just sat there, eyes lowered, slowly shaking his head, rubbing his palms together. Marcus glanced over at Vanessa who looked both sad and relieved, and a little worried. He could relate. Telling his father the truth had been hard as hell, but he knew that living a lie would have been so much worse. It would have weighed on him the rest of his life.

"Would you please say something?" Marcus said. "Tell me what you're thinking."

His father finally looked over to him. "I find it ironic, I guess."

"Ironic how?"

"Because I have a secret, too."

"The reason you couldn't marry me?" Vanessa asked.

He nodded. "Because I'm engaged to someone else."

For a second Vanessa just sat there, looking dumbfounded, then she laughed.

"You think that's funny?" Marcus asked.

"Not funny ha-ha, but funny ironic. I guess because I

was so focused on Marcus, I didn't really see it. Suddenly everything makes sense."

Marcus was completely confused. "See *what?*"

"Why he stopped Skyping, why his calls were less frequent and increasingly impersonal. You were falling in love with her."

"It was difficult to look you in the eye," his father said, "to just hear your voice. I felt so guilty. I knew I had to end it but I didn't want to hurt you."

"I know exactly what you mean!" she said. "You have no idea how relieved I felt when you said we couldn't Skype anymore. I was so scared that the second you saw my face you would know what I was thinking."

Gabriel smiled. "Me, too."

"Excuse me," Marcus said, raising his hand. "Would someone like to tell me who is it that you were falling in love with?"

Vanessa looked at him like he was a moron, and right now, he sort of felt like one. "It's your Aunt Trina."

Marcus turned to his father, and could see by the look on his face that it was true. "You're engaged to *Trina?*"

He nodded. "Almost losing her opened my eyes to my feelings for her."

He and Aunt Trina had always been close, but Marcus honestly believed their relationship had been platonic.

"We didn't mean for it to happen," his father said. "But after spending so much time together, we just knew. I guess you can understand how that goes."

"When mother was still alive, did you and Trina...?

"Marcus, *no!* Of course not. I loved your mother. I *still* love her. And until recently I never thought of Trina as anything but a friend. I'm still not sure what happened, what changed, I just know that it's right." He turned to Vanessa. "I was going to tell you this, and apologize profusely for dragging you and your daughter halfway around the world, and for making promises I couldn't keep. It's not that I don't care for you deeply. It's because of you that I was able to open up my heart again. I was so lonely, and unhappy, and then I met you and for the first time in months I felt alive again. And hopeful. I wanted to hold on to that feeling, but deep down I think I knew that it wasn't going to last. I knew that we would never love each other the way a wife and husband should."

"I wanted to love you that way," she said. "I wanted to be that woman."

"You are that woman, Vanessa." He looked to Marcus and smiled. "Just not for me."

"So, you're not angry?" Marcus asked.

"When I'm guilty of the same thing? You two love each other. And you were going to forsake your feelings to protect mine."

"Well, that was the plan," Vanessa said, shooting Marcus a look, but she was smiling.

"Then how could I possibly be angry. Besides, I can't imagine anyone else I would rather have as my daughter-in-law. And at my age, I think I'd much prefer being a grandfather to Mia than a father. I know men my age do it all the time, but I'm just too old and set in my ways to start over."

And Marcus felt as if his life was just beginning. As if everything up until now had just been a rehearsal in preparation for the real thing. It was so perfect that for an instant he couldn't help wondering if they might still be asleep in his bed and this whole thing was just a dream.

Marcus reached his hand out to Vanessa, and she reached for him, and the instant their fingers touched he knew this was very real. And very right.

"Father, could you give us a moment alone?" he asked.

He rose from the sofa, a smile on his face. "Take all the time you need."

The door had barely closed behind him and Vanessa was in his arms.

Vanessa buried her face against Marcus's chest, holding on tight, almost afraid to believe this was really happening. That it had worked out. That somehow, by breaking the rules and doing the *wrong* thing, she got exactly what she wanted.

"Is it real?" she asked him. "Could we be that lucky?"

He tightened his hold on her and she heard him sigh. "It sure feels real to me. But I don't think luck had anything to do with it."

She pulled back to look at him. "Why did you do it, Marcus? You risked so much."

"When I thought of you and Mia leaving…I just couldn't stand it. And when I saw the way he greeted you, I just had a feeling that something was wrong."

"He still could have been angry."

"I know. But that was a chance I had to take."

"For me?"

"Of course." He touched her cheek. "I love you, Vanessa."

He'd said it before, but until now, she hadn't allowed herself to really believe it. It would have been too painful when he let her down. But now, all that love, all those feelings she had been holding back, welled up inside her and she couldn't have held them back if her life depended on it. "I love you, Marcus. So much. I honestly didn't know it was possible to feel this happy."

"Well, get used to it," he said, kissing her gently. "Because if you'll have me, I'm going to spend the rest of my life making sure you stay that way."

"That's a long time."

"Vanessa, to truly express how much I love you, how much I *need* you, it would take an eternity."

She smiled. "Then I guess I'll just have to take your word for it."

"Does that mean you'll stay here with me, that you'll be my wife and make me the happiest man alive?"

In all the different places she had lived, Vanessa had never felt as if she truly belonged, but here, in Varieo with Marcus, she knew without a doubt that she was finally home.

"Yes," she told him, never feeling more sure about anything in her life. "I definitely will."

* * * * *

REQUEST YOUR FREE BOOKS!

2 FREE NOVELS PLUS 2 FREE GIFTS!

Harlequin® Desire

ALWAYS POWERFUL, PASSIONATE AND PROVOCATIVE

YES! Please send me 2 FREE Harlequin Desire® novels and my 2 FREE gifts (gifts are worth about $10). After receiving them, if I don't wish to receive any more books, I can return the shipping statement marked "cancel." If I don't cancel, I will receive 6 brand-new novels every month and be billed just $4.30 per book in the U.S. or $4.99 per book in Canada. That's a saving of at least 14% off the cover price! It's quite a bargain! Shipping and handling is just 50¢ per book in the U.S. and 75¢ per book in Canada.* I understand that accepting the 2 free books and gifts places me under no obligation to buy anything. I can always return a shipment and cancel at any time. Even if I never buy another book, the two free books and gifts are mine to keep forever.

225/326 HDN FEF3

Name _____ (PLEASE PRINT)

Address _____ Apt. #

City _____ State/Prov. _____ Zip/Postal Code

Signature (if under 18, a parent or guardian must sign)

Mail to the **Reader Service:**

IN U.S.A.: P.O. Box 1867, Buffalo, NY 14240-1867
IN CANADA: P.O. Box 609, Fort Erie, Ontario L2A 5X3

Not valid for current subscribers to Harlequin Desire books.

**Want to try two free books from another line?
Call 1-800-873-8635 or visit www.ReaderService.com.**

* Terms and prices subject to change without notice. Prices do not include applicable taxes. Sales tax applicable in N.Y. Canadian residents will be charged applicable taxes. Offer not valid in Quebec. This offer is limited to one order per household. All orders subject to credit approval. Credit or debit balances in a customer's account(s) may be offset by any other outstanding balance owed by or to the customer. Please allow 4 to 6 weeks for delivery. Offer available while quantities last.

Your Privacy—The Reader Service is committed to protecting your privacy. Our Privacy Policy is available online at www.ReaderService.com or upon request from the Reader Service.

We make a portion of our mailing list available to reputable third parties that offer products we believe may interest you. If you prefer that we not exchange your name with third parties, or if you wish to clarify or modify your communication preferences, please visit us at www.ReaderService.com/consumerschoice or write to us at Reader Service Preference Service, P.O. Box 9062, Buffalo, NY 14269. Include your complete name and address.

HDES11B

♦ **Harlequin** *Blaze*

red-hot reads

This navy lieutenant is about to get a blast from the past…and start thinking about the future.

Joanne Rock

captivates with another installment of

Men Out of Uniform

Five years ago, photojournalist Stephanie Rosen was kidnapped in a foreign country. Now, with her demons firmly behind her she is ready to move on…and to rev up her sex life! There's only one man she wants, friend and old flame, navy lieutenant Daniel Murphy. Their one night of passion years ago still leaves Stephanie breathless, and with Daniel on leave she's determined to give him a homecoming to remember.

FULL SURRENDER

Available this September wherever books are sold!

Enjoy this sneak peek of USA TODAY *bestselling author*
Maureen Child's newest title
UP CLOSE AND PERSONAL

Available September 2012 from Harlequin® Desire!

"**L**aura, I know you're in there!"

Ronan Connolly pounded on the bright blue front door, then paused to listen. Not a sound from inside the house, though he knew too well that Laura was in there. Hell, he could practically *feel* her standing just on the other side of the damned door.

He glanced at her car parked alongside the house, then glared again at the still-closed front door.

"You won't convince me you're not at home. Your car is parked in the street, Laura."

Her voice came then, muffled but clear. "It's a driveway in America, Ronan. You're not in Ireland, remember?"

"More's the pity." He scrubbed one hand across his face and rolled his eyes in frustration. If they were in Ireland right now, he'd have half the village of Dunley on his side and he'd bloody well get her to open the door.

"I heard that," she said.

Grinding his teeth together, he counted to ten. Then did it a second time. "Whatever the hell you want to call it, Laura, your car is *here* and so are you. Why not open the door and we can talk this out. Together. In private."

"I've got nothing to say to you."

He laughed shortly. That would be a first indeed, he told himself. A more opinionated woman he had never met. He had to admit, he had enjoyed verbally sparring with her. He admired a quick mind and a sharp tongue. He'd admired her even more once he'd gotten her into his bed.

He glanced down at the dozen red roses he held clutched in his right hand and called himself a damned fool for thinking this woman would be swayed by pretty flowers and a smooth speech. Hell, she hadn't even *seen* the flowers yet. At this rate, she never would.

Huffing out an impatient breath, he lowered his voice. "You know why I'm here. Let's get it done and have it over then."

There was a moment's pause, as if she were thinking about what he'd said. Then she spoke up again. "You can't have him."

"What?"

"You heard me."

Ronan narrowed his gaze fiercely on the door as if he could see through the panel to the woman beyond. "Aye, I heard you. Though, I don't believe it. I've come for what's mine, Laura, and I'm not leaving until I have it."

Will Ronan get what he's come for?

Find out in Maureen Child's new title
UP CLOSE AND PERSONAL

Available September 2012 from Harlequin® Desire!

The scandal continues
in The Santina Crown miniseries
with *USA TODAY* bestselling author

Sarah Morgan

Second in line to the throne, Matteo Santina
knows a thing or two about keeping his cool under
pressure. But when pop star singer Izzy Jackson
shows up to her sister's wedding and makes
a scandalous scene that goes against all royal
protocol, Matteo whisks her offstage, into his limo
and straight to his luxury palazzo…. Rumor has it
that they have yet to emerge!

DEFYING THE PRINCE

Available August 21 wherever books are sold!

www.Harlequin.com

HP13090

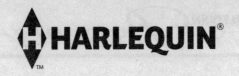

SO YOU THINK YOU CAN WRITE

Harlequin and Mills & Boon are joining forces in a global search for new authors.

In September 2012 we're launching our biggest contest yet—with the prize of being published by the world's leader in romance fiction!

Look for more information on our website, **www.soyouthinkyoucanwrite.com**

So you think you can write? Show us!